Thunder Ice

Alison Acheson

Coteau Books

Edited by Barbara Sapergia.
Cover painting by Ward Schell.
Cover and book design by Ruth Linka.
Typeset by Ruth Linka.
Printed and bound in Canada.

The author would like to thank her mother for support and reading, Gerrie Noble for research suggestions, and Joan Hebden for answers.

The publisher gratefully acknowledges the financial assistance of the Saskatchewan Arts Board, the Canada Council, the Department of Canadian Heritage, and the City of Regina Arts Commission.

Canadian Cataloguing in Publication Data

Acheson, Alison, 1964-
 Thunder ice
 ISBN 1-55050-105-4
I. Title.
PS8551.C44T48 1996 jC813'.54 C96-920061-7
PZ7.A34Th

COTEAU BOOKS
401-2206 Dewdney Avenue
Regina, Saskatchewan
S4R 1H3

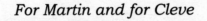

For Martin and for Cleve

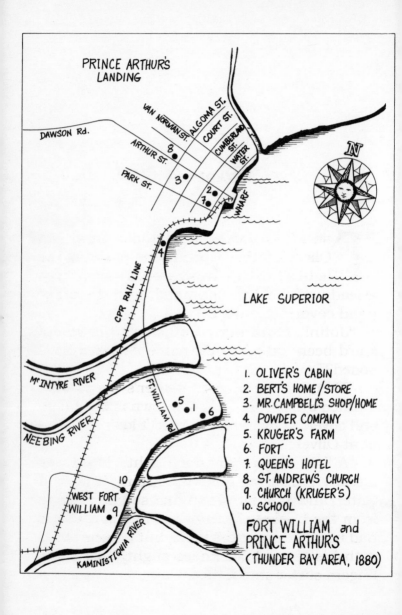

PRINCE ARTHUR'S
LANDING

DAWSON Rd.

VAN NORMAN ST.
ALGOMA ST.
COURT ST.
CUMBERLAND ST.
WATER ST.
ARTHUR ST.
PARK ST.
WHARF

8

3

2
7

4

CPR RAIL LINE

LAKE SUPERIOR

McINTYRE RIVER

NEEBING RIVER

FT. WILLIAM RD.

5
1
6

10

WEST FORT
WILLIAM
9

KAMINISTIQUIA RIVER

N

1. OLIVER'S CABIN
2. BERT'S HOME/STORE
3. MR. CAMPBELL'S SHOP/HOME
4. POWDER COMPANY
5. KRUGER'S FARM
6. FORT
7. QUEEN'S HOTEL
8. ST. ANDREW'S CHURCH
9. CHURCH (KRUGER'S)
10. SCHOOL

FORT WILLIAM and
PRINCE ARTHUR'S
(THUNDER BAY AREA, 1880)

Chapter 1

THE HEAVY MAPLE DOOR SWUNG OPEN, AND Oliver's father stood there, blocking the light of the morning sun. His cap was already off, held in one hand, and the other hand covered his nose.

"John!" Mum moved quickly from where she'd been sitting at the table. "What's happened?"

"There's been a fight." Father's words were muffled by his hand. He sat down at the table, still covering his nose. He didn't look at Mum, or at Oliver.

"A fight? John, you don't fight." Mum was already preparing a cloth, dipping it in cold water, and wrapping it around scoops of snow from the bucket she kept by the door. Oliver had been sitting at the table, but now he stood with his legs apart, knees slightly bent, his fingers curled into fists.

Mum didn't notice his fists. "You don't fight," she repeated softly and stepped towards Father.

Behind her, Oliver stalked to the coat peg on the back of the door. He barely heard his mother's words. He wanted to find the person who'd knuckled his father's nose. What he would do when he found him – whoever he was – he didn't know, but he could imagine.

"Here, you! Take this! And this!" Oliver's fists would fly like never before, with all the energy of a hunting hound let loose. He could almost feel the flesh under his hand, hear the sound of the strike. How dare someone hit his father. His father, who'd never struck anyone in his life! How dare....

Oliver was suddenly conscious of Mum, staring at his hands. He shoved the fists into his pockets. Mum looked like she might start crying, and Oliver heard the sound of a deep sob. But it wasn't coming from his mother. He looked at his father and saw a tear on his cheek. The first that Oliver'd ever seen there. Then Father looked directly at him.

"I'm sorry, son. I've tried to teach you to be a peacemaker, and I can't even be one myself."

Oliver didn't say anything. He felt his fists still clenched in his pockets. They didn't feel like the hands of a peacemaker.

He wouldn't have known what to say

anyway. This was the first time something like this had ever happened.

"It's this place!" said Mum, and she sounded angry. "It's this wild country we've come to, and these wretched towns. So much anger and competition. Who did you fight with?"

Oliver's father finally took his hand away from his face and put both of his hands flat on the table top. He stared at them for a long moment as if he didn't know how it was they'd come to be connected to the rest of his body. His head bowed and he said the name so quietly that Oliver and his mother could barely hear it.

"Will."

"Your brother?" Mum whispered. Uncle Will, thought Oliver, and his fists loosened suddenly, his need for revenge gone. He tried to imagine his father and his favourite uncle fighting, hurting each other, and he couldn't, yet the proof was right in front of him. His father's nose, bloodied and bruised.

Earlier in December, Uncle Will and Father had argued for the first time. Oliver thought of that now and tried to remember what the argument had been about. Oh yes, the row of books that was always on the mantel, books that Oliver's father had bound back home. Father had asked Uncle Will what sort of price the books might fetch if he were to sell them, and Uncle Will had leaped up from the table.

"You can't sell those books!"

It was the first time Oliver had heard his uncle's voice raised.

"I don't *want* to sell my books," Father had said.

"Then don't." And Uncle Will cracked his fist onto the table.

That was it until Oliver and his brother and sisters were in the loft, supposed to be asleep. But Oliver heard the men talk on into the night about money and work and this place they'd come to.

"Surely you knew you wouldn't be binding books here," Uncle Will said.

"No," Oliver's father said. "No – I didn't know that. I was hoping, I suppose."

They talked on as Oliver drifted to sleep. Their voices slowly warmed and grew and then there were angry words rising upstairs.

And now this. A fight with fists.

Mum looked miserable. "What are we going to do?"

It wasn't a strange question. Aunt Emily was Mum's closest friend. Cousin Bert was Oliver's. And until today, Father and Uncle Will had been as close as two brothers can be.

"Perhaps you can work this out," Mum said.

"Perhaps," Father said, but with little hope. He reached for the dripping cloth in Mum's hands, stood up, and filled it with snow himself.

Bert. Oliver had to see Bert. *They* could work this out. They wouldn't allow this fight of their fathers to affect *their* friendship. Their friendship was stronger than that. They could find out what their fathers had fought over and repair whatever it was. Things would be just fine by the time Oliver and Bert were finished!

Oliver couldn't imagine life without Bert. Not that Oliver didn't have enough family with one brother and three sisters, but Bert was special. They were the same age and they'd shared a bunk on the ship. They knew everything about each other. The only thing they didn't like about each other was that Bert lived in Prince Arthur's Landing, and Oliver lived in Fort William, and their homes were four miles apart. They'd found a couple of short cuts off the main trail, but still the trip took more than an hour on foot, and not much less on Old Mac, the horse.

Oliver could reach the Landing before dinner time if he started out now.

"Father?" His father barely moved his head, but Oliver knew he was listening. "May I have Old Mac for the afternoon?" He hoped his father wouldn't ask where he was going.

He didn't. When he heard Old Mac's name a strange look came over his face. "No – I'm afraid you can't. I'm going to take him into town later." He didn't say why he was taking the horse to town, or even which town – the Town Plot of West Fort William or the Landing – and Oliver didn't ask. After all, his father hadn't asked Oliver where he was going.

In his cotton food sack, Oliver packed a large piece of venison and a roll of bread spread thickly with pink pin cherry jelly. He put on the heavy wool sweater Mum had knit for him.

As he set out, he decided to go by the lakeshore, instead of by the road. In the Bay, there was a thick armour of ice, and there was a stillness about it that he liked, though the lake wind was cold on this, the last day of 1879.

It was early afternoon when Oliver walked into the town of Prince Arthur's Landing. It was a busy place – almost a thousand people lived there – and there was always a feeling of excitement on the streets, usually because of the silver mines. The Shuniah mine was the closest. If Oliver and Bert stood on the sill of Bert's bedroom window and looked north of town, they could see the rooftops of the mine buildings. Once they'd started out to see the mine, but Uncle Will had caught up with them just as they reached the site. "The mine shafts are dangerous," he'd said. "You might fall in." And that was that. They'd headed home.

Businessmen stood in groups outside the hotels and boarding houses and they talked about diggings and banks. Oliver's father called these men "gamblers," and Oliver could tell, just by the way his father said "gamblers," that he didn't approve of them. It seemed to Oliver that his father didn't approve of anything in the Landing. Maybe that's why Oliver's family had stayed in Fort William when Uncle Will had decided to move Bert and Aunt Emily to Prince Arthur's Landing.

Oliver liked his home in Fort William. He liked the marsh in summer, with cranberries and saskatoons, and the lowing of cows, and the broken old fort nearby, still protected by faltering palisades. And he liked the Kaministiquia River with its heavy winter ice and the sound of sleighs running over it.

But when he was in the Landing he always walked a little faster and raised his head a bit higher. Smells of hotcakes and frying lake fish – trout or pike – wafted from the hotel kitchens, and fiddle music crept from under the doors of saloons. At the foot of Arthur Street was the lake, and in winter, the place where boys and girls skated. On particularly cold afternoons they warmed themselves by eating hot roasted potatoes.

On Arthur Street, women paraded in hats and some men wore beards to their waists.

7

Oliver liked listening to the miners – they talked so roughly and used words that Oliver wasn't supposed to use. But he never stood too close – they spit chewing tobacco!

Bert's house was on Arthur Street. It was on the second level over the dry goods store that Uncle Will owned and there were two doors into their home. One was at the back of the building, at the top of some stairs, and the other entrance was through the rear of the store. Oliver hoped that Bert would be outside. He didn't want to run into Uncle Will.

Oliver started around the corner to the stairs.

"Oliver! Pssstt!" That was Bert's voice.

Oliver turned. His cousin's hand was beckoning from a clump of snow-covered cedar trees. Before going towards the cedars, Oliver looked around him. It seemed the thing to do with Bert hiding so mysteriously. He had to crawl under the branches and when he did, he found himself inside a small but open area. At another time of year it would be quite dark inside the green cave, but with the snow, it was bright.

"I cut a few branches off yesterday," Bert said, showing Oliver where he'd used the hatchet. The branches were laid on the ground. There was very little snow inside the cluster of cedars, the branches were so close together.

Oliver could even feel the cushion of old cedar bits. It was spongy and rather comfortable. He sat down next to Bert.

"I've spent a lot of time here today," said Bert.

This was his way of telling Oliver that he too was upset about the fight.

"What are we going to do?" asked Oliver. He didn't look at Bert, but stared out underneath the branches at the feet of humans and dogs, and at horses' hooves and sleigh runners on the street.

"We've got to talk some sense into your father," said Bert. He too watched the passersby.

Oliver turned and stared at his cousin. Had he heard correctly?

"What's wrong with my father?" he asked slowly.

But Bert didn't seem to hear him. He'd ducked his head lower and was scrutinizing the trouser legs of someone standing just in front of their trees. "Look!" he whispered. "It's Mr. Phillips. He's one of the men who fought for the railway to run through the Landing."

Oliver had heard about Mr. Phillips, but at that moment he couldn't care less. There were other, more important things – like his father.

"What about my father?" He pulled on Bert's sleeve.

Bert finally paid attention to Oliver. "He's a stubborn goat, my pa says."

Oliver thought for a word to describe his father. "He's not stubborn – he's *persistent!*"

Bert laughed, and Oliver wondered if he took this fight seriously after all. And he had to admit to himself that his father was stubborn. Maybe if Bert realized how stubborn, he wouldn't be laughing. And if he were to look at Oliver's face he'd know how worried Oliver was. This fight was serious. Nothing like it had ever happened before. His father never fought. He didn't even like to argue. In fact, he usually avoided anything that was the least bit like a confrontation. And here was Bert, laughing.

"Persistent?" said Bert. "You think your father is *persistent?* My pa says he'd need a railway engine to smash through your father's pride."

"Why would he want to?"

Bert became quiet. "I don't know."

"You don't know what?"

"I don't know exactly what the fight was about. I only know that they hollered a lot and my pa has a black eye and your father has a bloody nose."

"If you don't know what the fight was about, why are you saying that my father is stubborn? That's just something your father said...." Oliver was starting to feel angry all over again.

Bert wasn't laughing now. "Your father is stubborn and you know it! Remember? It was his idea to come to this country. He insisted this would be the best thing we could possibly do. My mum's wanted to go home ever since we arrived here – no, since we walked up the gangway onto the ship in Liverpool."

"No, she hasn't!"

"Yes, she has – your mum too!"

"No, she hasn't!" Oliver pulled at a twig that kept catching his cap. He broke it off with a snap.

"Hey! Why'd you do that? I left that branch there to hang my cap on."

Oliver twisted the soft cedar twig.

"I wish you hadn't broken it off," said Bert.

"It's just a dumb branch – and my mum doesn't want to go home. She tells my father she's happy here." Oliver didn't mention what his mother had said about the wretched and wild towns they lived in.

"She says she's happy just because she *can't* go back." Bert was shouting now.

"Could too, if she wanted to – I tell you, she doesn't want to," Oliver shouted back.

"Your father isn't working – how would he pay for a ticket?"

"He'll find work."

The two boys stared at each other. Both were out of breath. Oliver shivered suddenly.

This wasn't supposed to happen. He'd come here to find out what had happened with his father, and now he and Bert were having an argument too. He opened his mouth. He meant for the words, "I'm sorry," to come out, but instead he sat there with a gaping mouth, then closed it. Bert was the person who'd said all the horrible things. Let him say sorry first.

Oliver pulled at the ends of the cedar twig and broke it in two. He threw the pieces down onto the floor of branches and scrabbled out from under the trees. He stood up on the other side, brushing snow off his trousers. He couldn't see Bert.

But he could hear his voice: "Your father is the most stubborn old goat, and your mum does want to go home." He wasn't shouting now. His voice was rather quiet and Oliver could feel him looking right through the thick mesh of branches.

"Stubborn? You think my father is stubborn? I'll show you stubborn! You've never seen *my* stubborn. Why..." Oliver tried to think of the best example of how stubborn he could be. "I'll never speak to you again!" Then he turned and walked away, even swaggered slightly.

Chapter 2

O N THE WAY HOME THE WINTER SKY DARKENED. The food that Oliver had put in his sack was long gone. He'd eaten it on his way to the Landing and now he realized that he'd been counting on having dinner and being able to spend the night at his cousin's home as he usually did. And he'd expected to be the peacemaker between his father and his father's brother. His plans hadn't worked at all, and the empty feeling in his belly wasn't hunger alone.

The wind was strong, blowing off Lake Superior. Oliver walked quickly and passed the Powder Company – the first mile on the way home. He must have lost his woolen mittens along the way. He searched for them in his pockets, his food sack, inside his hat where he kept them sometimes. He watched for them on the path. Bert could have found them; Bert had a knack for finding things. Oliver tried to stop thinking about his cousin. Instead, he concentrated on trying to keep his hands warm. He shoved them into his pockets where they would stay warm, but that slowed his stride. So he swung his arms and pulled the cuffs of his sweater over his hands. His fingers, curled over the edges of the rough wool, felt like they were beginning to freeze. The mittens were his favourites.

The setting sun and the trees made long shadows. Oliver wished he had Old Mac – not only because he'd be so much faster, but because he knew the path so well, even in the dark. And Oliver could wrap his arms around the old horse's neck, warm his face in the rough strands of mane, and close his eyes, pretend he was in bed with the goose down quilt. Perhaps he should turn back – maybe he and Bert could end this fight now. No, Oliver was quite sure that this fight was not going to end ever.

Another gust of wind from the lake caught Oliver's breath and whisked it away.

It was too late to go back anyway. He was already halfway. It would be completely dark soon – unless the wind was blowing in his favour and moved aside the clouds that trapped the light of the moon. He and his father had made this trip in moonlight. At least it was downhill and there was snow on the ground – that helped. It seemed to illuminate the path, and Oliver knew better than to step in the shadowy holes.

His father. For the first time in his life, Oliver felt angry with his father. Well, perhaps that was an exaggeration. He'd been angry with him before, but not like he was now.

Oliver stumbled over something – he couldn't see what it was in the tree shadow at his feet. He kicked whatever it was aside, and felt something else brush his toe. He kicked again. It was a branch, more awkward than heavy. He picked it up and threw it to the side of the path. "Go away!" he yelled after the branch. It crashed into the brush and an animal, probably a rabbit, scurried out. Oliver yelled again. He thought of the miners cursing on the streets of the Landing. "Damn!" he hollered.

He didn't feel like yelling after that. Suddenly he didn't even feel angry with his father. He thought of how Mum would be upset if she heard him curse, and he muttered, "Sorry, Mum. It just came out."

Yelling had warmed him, or perhaps made him forget the cold. And he'd been moving quickly. He'd be home soon.

Bert and Oliver had found a short cut to this part of the trail not long ago, and now Oliver wondered whether to use it. It would make his journey shorter by almost a quarter of an hour, yet it was so much darker and overgrown than the trail he was now on.

His teeth were tap-dancing in the cold, and his toes were sleeping. He decided to take the short cut.

A few minutes later, he realized his mistake. It was so dark that he had to stretch his arms out in front of him to feel for the trees that grew tall over his head and blocked whatever moonlight might sneak through. Here, even the snow did not brighten his way, and the untouched surface was frozen hard, unlike the trampled path he'd left behind. His feet slid as if he was on skate blades. There were fallen logs and he stumbled and slipped and finally began to drag his feet so that he could feel his way. At this rate it would take an hour.

Then he heard a familiar sound. A tired neigh. Old Mac. The horse was standing still in front of him and must have heard him. Oliver reached out toward the horse. "Mac!" He grasped the animal's mane and pulled himself up. He wrapped his hands in the warmth of Mac's mane. "Take me home, Old Mac."

The horse neighed, turned, and began to plod homeward. Oliver could hear frozen snow breaking under Mac's hooves. Oliver kept his head down, out of the wind. His body warmed with the horse moving under him.

What had Old Mac been doing out on the

trail? he wondered suddenly. On a night like this, his father would have put Mac in the shed. True, Old Mac would have found it easy to push the door open, but he'd been with the Tate family for over a year – almost as long as they'd been in Canada – and he'd never wandered off before.

Oliver lifted his head. At the foot of the sloping path, he could see the light from the kitchen window of the Kruger farm now. Oliver's home was a small rented cabin on the back property of the Krugers. It was close. Mac knew it and quickened his pace until they reached home, and then the horse stopped outside the nearby shed and waited for Oliver to open the door.

Both of Oliver's parents stood in the doorway as he neared the cabin, and little Hannah peered from where she crouched between her father's legs.

"Olver's home!" she announced the arrival of her favourite brother.

Mum rushed forward with a blanket she'd been holding, and wrapped it around Oliver's shoulders. Hannah held onto him until Mum led her away to tuck her into bed.

His father remained in the doorway, with his face in the shadows, almost hiding the bruise beside his swollen nose. As Oliver passed by him, he asked, "How did you come home?"

"I found Old Mac on the trail. Or maybe it was the other way around: Old Mac found me."

His father looked toward the shed before he spoke. "I thought I saw you putting him away for the night." He rubbed his nose and seemed about to speak again, but instead winced in pain.

"I thought perhaps you'd sent Mac out for me?"

"No – I didn't." His father stared at him for a moment. "No. He must have gotten lost. I went back to Prince Arthur's this afternoon and took Old Mac with me." He paused. "I left him there with Mr. Phillips."

"You left him with Mr. Phillips?" Oliver repeated.

"Yes – I sold him to Mr. Phillips. I guess he ran away. I'll have to take him back tomorrow."

"You sold Old Mac?" Oliver whispered.

"I had to." His father turned away and stood at the stove ladling soup into a bowl for Oliver.

Oliver couldn't help looking towards the mantel to see if the row of books was still there.

The mantel was clear.

"Here," said father. He placed the bowl of soup on the table.

But Oliver wasn't hungry any more.

Chapter 3

OLIVER DREAMED OF A DARK GREY WALL. THE wall moved alongside him. He could have reached for it from where he lay, but he didn't. Instead he pushed himself deeper into his mattress as the wall curved out over him. Maybe it would crush him.

Then it seemed to move up and down, as if it were floating. Of course! He was back in Liverpool. The wall must be the side of one of the great steamships. He should have known it was Liverpool from the sounds of the voices: more voices than there were in all of Canada, it seemed.

If this was Liverpool, then Bert must be here. They always waited together for this ship – the Majestic – to come in with its loads of timber from Canada.

Oliver peered from his warm bed, up the grey side of the ship. The ship was pulling out, not in. Maybe Bert was up there, on the deck, waving. Maybe that was why, through all the voices, all the shouts of dock hands, Oliver could hear Bert's voice calling him.

"Ollie!" came the voice. "Ollie?"

But we aren't talking any more, remember? thought Oliver. We've been on this ship already, we've seen Canadian timber before it's cut. What do you want with me, Bert?

He turned away from the wall of the ship and was amazed how easy it was to turn away. Why hadn't he thought to do that before? When he thought he was going to be crushed?

He walked away down the dock – or was it the bridge over the Neebing River? – but the voice followed him.

"Ollie – over here!"

Now the voice sounded scared. Oliver kept walking.

"Ollie!"

He stopped.

"Ollie!"

"Where are you, Bert?" Oliver shouted. He stood still.

"Over here. I'm caught." The voice seemed farther away.

"Where?" Oliver began to run towards the sound.

"Here."

"I can barely hear you – yell, Bert, yell!"

Oliver's breathing was louder than all the other sounds, louder than Bert's voice, almost gone now.

"Where are you?" he shouted again into the sudden darkness of the grey Liverpool sky – or was it the wall of the ship again upon him?

He had to find Bert.

Then he saw a boot – Bert's boot, surely – protruding from behind a wooden packing crate. He reached down to pull at it.

And awoke to find himself shivering on the floor beside his bed, his own boot in his hands. He'd pulled it from behind the bedpost, where he tucked them at night.

He clutched the boot close to him and his mind darkened with a feeling that all was not right with the world. Something, perhaps everything, was quite wrong with it.

Then he remembered the day before. He remembered his father's bruised face, and then Bert. Not Bert in Liverpool, calling to him, but Bert under the cedar trees.

During the night the winter air had crept through the chinks in the wall and the floor was a cold place.

"Oliver!" Mum called to him from the kitchen. "Breakfast!"

Oliver sat up, still holding the boot. The other beds in the loft were empty. Eliza and Alberta's big square bed that Father had made;

the woven twine that supported their quilts creaked every time one of his sisters moved, and Alberta moved often! And little Gavin's bed, which was the one trunk the family owned. It had held most of their belongings on the ship.

This morning, it was only Oliver's breath that rose in the cold air.

His thoughts moved on to Old Mac. His father was probably up – he was an early riser. Perhaps he'd taken Mac already.

Oliver rushed to put a flannel shirt over his woolen drawers, and because he rushed, he managed to turn the sleeves inside out, and twist the back of the shirt so that the whole chore of dressing took twice as long as it ought to have. Heavy wool pants and knitted wool socks followed the shirt. He liked the warming, scratchy feel of wool. Perhaps it could banish the chill he'd picked up the night before. He climbed down the ladder to breakfast.

Hannah stood at the foot of the ladder as he reached the last rung.

"Olver!" she shouted, and grabbed his hand to lead him to the breakfast table.

Eliza looked at him with curiosity, but didn't ask where he'd been the evening before. Alberta did, though. "Where were you? It was bath night!"

Gavin ignored his brother and continued eating his breakfast. Food was always his first priority.

Mum noticed Oliver staring at Father's place. "He's gone to the Town Plot to see about work," she said.

"Old Mac?" asked Oliver.

"He's in the shed."

He wasn't too late then. He pushed the last corner of crust into his mouth, wiped his hands on his trouser legs, and walked across the room to reach for his jacket hanging on a wooden peg near the door.

"Oliver," Mum spoke softly.

Oliver turned towards her.

"Oliver, your father wants you to take the horse to Mr. Phillips."

He turned away quickly, angry, grabbed his jacket from the peg, and went outside without putting it on. Mum called as he hurried to the shed, but he ignored her. How could his father expect him to do such a thing? Old Mac was special!

Yet Oliver had to admit that, much as he cared for the horse, Mac wasn't worth much to anyone else. In fact, that was what worried him about this deal his father had made. He didn't want to imagine what Mr. Phillips wanted with Mac. People did horrible things to old animals.

And why Mr. Phillips? His name was not a favourite in Fort William. Mr. Phillips was part of a group of men who'd tried since before 1875 to have the Canadian Pacific Railway stationed at Prince Arthur's Landing. In Fort William, another group had persuaded the government that their town was the superior choice. But the Landing would not give up. It was an old battle.

Oliver had heard all about this from Uncle Will. His father tried to ignore such controversies and stayed clear of the competition between the two towns.

A gust of air blew the shed door closed behind him, but Old Mac didn't even raise his head from his solid munch, munch of hay.

"Hey, old bloke!" murmured Oliver softly. The horse looked up and snorted an answer. Oliver moved until he was next to Mac, then leaned against the big warm body.

The shed was cosy with the horse's steamy breath and with the mounds of hay in three of the four corners. Oliver sat on the only tied bale and tried to explain to Old Mac what it was he had to do.

"Phillips wants you," he began, and felt older saying "Phillips" without the Mister before it. "I don't know why, but he does want you." After that, Oliver wasn't sure what to say. Mac kept chewing, and finally Oliver stood and reached for the halter on the wall. He slipped it over the horse's head and led him outside. He'd ride without a saddle. There was no point in having to drag it back home.

He climbed onto the broad back of the horse and turned Mac to the northeast.

"Oliver," called Mum from behind him. She'd packed supper in his sack and was carrying his new Christmas present snowshoes. "You'll need these." She handed him the sack first, then the snowshoes, which he slung over his back. It was about time he tackled learning to walk with them, and with any luck they would make the trip home easier than it had been the day before.

Then Mum stood back. "I'll be sad to see him go." She looked from Old Mac to Oliver. "I know you will be too."

Oliver nodded sharply. He didn't want to think of Old Mac gone, or Mum sad. He pressed the horse's flank with his heels and they were away.

He didn't take the short cuts. Instead, as this was the last time he would be able to ride Mac, he took the path that followed the shoreline of the lake. He and Mac often used the path, particularly in summer. They had a special place, close to the Landing, a little flat beach, mossy in the summer, hidden from the wind in winter. There he would meet Bert, and they'd stop to eat or just daydream in silence. In winter, Mr. Meikle might be skating – he was a fancy skater – and Oliver and Bert would watch him etch circles and turns into the ice and spin on one spot. He was the finest skater in the country, many people said.

Today Oliver didn't stop for long; it was too cold. The lake was quiet in winter, ice thick and white, with wide ripples where the wind had shaped it as it froze. Every year, for months, it was like that. So solid nothing could break it except the end of winter. And even the end of winter couldn't break the ice: it had to persuade it gently, coaxing with the weak warmth of the spring sun, softening, melting, then finally it would crack, thin cracks, and crinkle and push to the shore.

Although Oliver missed the summer sound of water lapping, he preferred the ice. Once he'd used Scrawny Joe's dog team and sleigh – Joe worked for Uncle Will – and the dogs had pulled Oliver, skimming along with the hard sound of steel on ice. It had been a sunny day and the frosted surface sparkled. It seemed impossible that underneath was deep, black water. Oliver had come to Canada early one fall. This was now his second winter, and last year he'd decided the ice was one of the best parts of his new home. He'd never before seen anything like it. He knew that for some people in the towns – such as the businessmen – the ice signified a stopping of trade. Ships couldn't come into Thunder Bay and the area was cut off and isolated. That same isolation had affected his family: Oliver's father had had a bit of work at the dock, but with winter that had come to an end.

But Oliver came from a big city where he'd always felt crowded, and he rather liked the stillness of winter in the Bay. It made him feel like an adventurer. It made him feel solid, solid as that ice, and solid as the Sleeping Giant who lay behind the towns.

The mountainous Indian chief was unmoving in his rock cliffs. Oliver always felt his presence even as the chief slept. The people who'd lived the longest in this area – Thunder Bay – said it was the home of the Thunder God. Oliver suspected that the Giant was the Thunder God. Sometimes he had the feeling that one day the Sleeping Giant would awaken and roar in anger at the feuding towns – perhaps now at Oliver's own father. That thought made Oliver smile! But for now the Sleeping Giant was still and at peace with the land he protected.

Oliver was daydreaming and Mr. Phillips would be wondering where they were, so he and Mac continued until they were at the point where the rough path met the tamed roadway of the Landing's main street. Then Mac stopped entirely. Oliver dug his heels in until he knew Mac was in pain. He talked to him, putting his mouth to the flicking ear, but Mac shook his head. Oliver climbed down from the horse and tried to lead him, tugging on the reins, but Mac refused to move.

If this had been yesterday morning, he would have fetched Bert, and together they would have figured out this problem. Bert often had clever ideas. And when he didn't, he managed to find a few in Oliver's head that Oliver hadn't known were there.

Oliver couldn't help glancing up the street towards his cousin's home. He could see the clump of cedars from where he stood. He imagined Bert in their greenness at this very moment, but then he saw Bert himself come from behind the building and enter the dry goods store. Oliver turned away quickly.

"Come on, Old Mac!" He jerked the reins. The horse moved one small step, his four hooves pushing the snow into little piles before them. But that was it – one step – that was as far as he would go. Oliver sniffed. Was that a slight whiff of smoke? Usually Mac wasn't bothered by a bit of smoke from a chimney – it had to be more than that to affect the old horse. Oliver remembered the last time Mac had been near a fire – a small fire in some bush at the east side of Kruger's grazing land. Mac had gone quite mad and, later in the shed, had not stopped snorting and pushing at the door.

But perhaps Oliver was mistaken. He sniffed again. Nothing now.

There were a few tree stumps beside the

road, one sawed to a perfect height for sitting on. Oliver sat on the stump, a short distance from the stubborn or frightened horse, and he opened the sack his mother had prepared. He chewed slowly, half hoping the smell of food would lure the horse from his stance. But Mac remained where he stood at an invisible tethering pole, and the smell of still-warm bread didn't seem to reach him.

The cold, however, was pulling Oliver into its fingers. He shivered.

Maybe he would find Mr. Phillips. Or maybe he wouldn't. If Phillips wanted Old Mac, he could come and fetch the horse himself. Oliver smiled at the thought, but his smile was slow in the cold wind.

Why did Mr. Phillips want Mac?

Maybe he would find the man and ask him. "Why do you want my horse?"

And Phillips would reply ... what would he say?

It wasn't enough to sit and imagine answers. If Oliver was brave, he'd go and ask.

And when he'd found Mr. Phillips, and asked him, Oliver would say, "Well sir, that's nice and everything, but I'm afraid I can't let you take him. You see, Old Mac belongs to me, not my father, and besides, my family needs him. He's our transportation, and he's my friend."

Then Mr. Phillips would say, "Fine, boy, but in that case I believe you have some money that ought to be returned to me."

Of course! The money. How much had Mr. Phillips paid his father? Maybe Oliver could find a job, although that seemed unlikely. His father hadn't been able to. How could he? But if Oliver had a job, he could earn the money himself and buy back Old Mac. The thought was exciting. If only....

Oliver looked at Mac, stamping his feet in the loose snow, head down, trying to keep warm.

What was he going to do? A good boy – that is, a boy who would obey his father – would simply take the horse to the new owner. But Old Mac wasn't letting him do that.

An adventurer would turn the horse around and ride him away, away from both towns, and together they'd find a new life. Oliver liked this idea. Maybe they could set out on the Dawson trail, the trail that led West to Red River. Of course, Oliver and Old Mac wouldn't go all the way to Red River. They'd stop somewhere and find work – or at least Oliver would find work – and he'd send money to his family so that his father wouldn't need to sell Mac. Yes. And when he returned home – perhaps his employer could spare him over Easter – it would be to the greeting of Hannah's proud eyes.

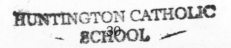

Old Mac had finally moved and was now nudging Oliver's elbow. "Let's get moving," he seemed to say. "Stop your daydreaming."

Oliver turned his sack inside out and shook crumbs onto the snow. Five hungry-looking pigeons flew from where they'd been waiting in the birches and landed at his feet.

No, today he would be neither a good boy, nor an adventurer. Even if he'd wanted to take Mac to Mr. Phillips, he couldn't have. And he didn't want to. But he couldn't take Old Mac and run away.

Instead, he pulled on Mac's reins, and began to lead him back home. Oliver was too cold to ride. Maybe walking would warm him up a bit. He pulled his muffler higher around his face.

His father had sold Mac; let his father take the horse to Phillips.

Oliver was a quarter of a mile from the Landing when he saw another traveller. Someone on a horse, someone with his muffler wrapped high around his face as well, his head bent down to avoid the wind. It wasn't until the traveller was quite close that Oliver saw it was Mr. Phillips himself. Only then did Oliver realize how much he'd wanted not to turn Mac over to this man.

He'd met Mr. Phillips only twice before, but he wasn't the kind of person one forgot. He had great hairy brows that were now covered with icy frost, icy to match his blue eyes. He had a full beard and mustache, also hoary with frost. There wasn't really much of his face to be seen, except those eyes. Those eyes that now scrutinized Oliver and Old Mac.

"That'll be my horse now, won't it?" A voice came from behind the frosted face.

Oliver wished he was riding Mac instead of standing beside him. He could dig his heels in and off they'd go.

"I was just out at your place," boomed Phillips. Mac stepped back.

"Your mother said I'd find you on your way to Prince Arthur's?" Mr. Phillips's sentence ended in a question mark, but Oliver didn't answer.

He knew that it was time to hand the reins of Old Mac over to this man, but he couldn't. He stood there, and because he didn't want to look into those icy eyes, he shuffled his feet in the snow and looked down at his boots, peeking through white powder. He could feel Phillips's hand reaching out, and still Oliver didn't pass the reins to him.

Maybe Old Mac would refuse to move for Mr. Phillips too.

But that was not to be. The horse must have sensed that this was a battle he couldn't win, and when Oliver finally put the worn leather reins into the gloved hand that waited, the horse began to move away, though slowly.

Oliver stood and watched them until they were out of sight. Then he turned to go. And realized he'd left his snowshoes at the stump where he'd eaten lunch.

Chapter 4

THE SNOWSHOES WEREN'T THERE, BUT THERE WERE tracks: big bootprints that stopped at the stump and turned around. Whoever belonged to the prints probably had the snowshoes.

Oliver followed the prints – right past his cousin's house. He tried not to look up, but then there he was, standing by the cedars, looking up at the narrow window high in the bald front of the dry goods store. Behind that window was Aunt Emily's front room. It was the room that Bert and Oliver were not supposed to be in – except on Sundays, when they were allowed to sit quietly on the sofa, which they never did. Sometimes, when Bert was waiting for Oliver, he waited in that room, watching from the window. Aunt Emily seemed not to notice this. But today the window was like a blank eye, staring at Oliver.

It wasn't that Oliver expected to see Bert looking back at him through the glass – Bert was still in the store, no doubt – but the empty window was like a mirror of Oliver's sudden and overwhelming loneliness.

Oliver told himself that he didn't want to see Bert, he didn't want to speak to him. Couldn't, not after yesterday, when he'd threatened never to speak to him again. And then, there was Bert, in the store, moving towards the glass door, moving towards Oliver. Too late for Oliver to move out of sight. Bert walked through the door and the bells that hung over the door jangled as it closed. Oliver felt the air stop in his lungs. Bert hardly looked at him: his eyes shifted from Oliver's quickly. But Oliver knew that Bert had seen him standing there. If there was a moment when Oliver could have said something – something about forgetting yesterday, something about being sorry – this was it. And then that moment was gone and Bert had disappeared around the corner of his home, and Oliver was left in the grey cold, still trying to breathe.

He told himself it was all right – he hadn't come to say he was sorry, he hadn't wanted to speak with Bert anyway – but he'd never felt so alone in his life. Nothing could compare to this – not even when he'd gotten lost while exploring on the ship, and fallen through a hole in the floor. He'd thought that no one would ever find him and that had been terrible. But this was different, because here he was – he wasn't lost – and he was so alone.

He found the bootprints again, and followed them down Arthur Street.

All along the street, people were removing signs of the New Year's Eve festivities the night before. Storefronts and boarding houses had been decorated with pine boughs and bunting – long strips of woolen fabric, red and purple, wrapped around porch posts and doorways. Shopkeepers shouted to each other across the street. "Happy New Year!" A few snowballs passed over Oliver's head. A New Year was always something to look forward to – a time to start over. A time to forget the mistakes of the past year and resolve to do better in the new.

"It's too late for me! I've already started the New Year horribly!" Oliver bent to the ground for a handful of snow, shaped it, packed it hard, and threw it back in the direction of his cousin's home. It burst onto the roof, right about where Bert's bedroom was, and left a white blot. Had Bert heard it? Even though Oliver didn't want to think about it, he remembered last winter. Bert and he, against Eliza and Alberta, waging snow battle from behind thick walls of the white stuff. Hannah running from one blockade to the other, one minute wanting to be on Oliver's side, and the next minute wanting to be with her sisters.

For the prospectors and businessmen of Prince Arthur's Landing, a New Year meant more time to gamble with, and the dream of finding another cache of the earth's glittering silver harvest.

In Fort William, there'd probably been a party at the old Hudson's Bay Post. Oliver imagined the festivities there: quiet, organized, people sitting, dancing, eating, sitting again. Then again, maybe they'd left the dancing to one of the hotels at the Town Plot. There would have been none of the noisy jubilance he imagined in the Landing. Oliver passed by a saloon with doors wide open. The people inside, mostly men, seemed not to notice the cold. Some were dancing to fiddle music, a few even sweating.

Someone with a bass voice began to sing "Auld Lang Syne" – *Should auld acquaintance be forgot* ... but another voice shouted the singer down.

"It's over, lad! Pipe down!" Others joined in the roar that followed, and the singer quit.

Oliver had stopped outside the open doorway. He could see Miss Darbyshire in the dim saloon. She was dancing, and she held her dress up and kicked her legs so that he could even see one of her knees. The cold didn't seem to bother her at all. He moved closer to the open doorway.

"Young Oliver!" There was a hoarse holler from across the snowy street. "Young Oliver, put your eyes back in your head, and move yourself over here!"

Oliver recognized that voice. Mr. Campbell, the blacksmith. Once, and only once, he'd caught Oliver and Bert outside Miss Darbyshire's window – they'd heard that she was not too particular with her curtains – and Mr. Campbell would never let either boy forget it.

Mr. Campbell seemed to know exactly when and where someone was doing something, and more often than not, something he shouldn't be doing.

He'd caught Billy B. coming out of the Thunder Bay mine after a day's work, with his pockets full of silver bits, and he knew the places the Landing's children went when they dared to miss school.

People feared Mr. Campbell because of this ability of his – this ability to see what you were doing. He even seemed to know what you were thinking. Oliver tried always to stay out of Mr. Campbell's way, and he'd never again stood under Miss Darbyshire's window.

But there was another reason that people in Prince Arthur's Landing didn't like the blacksmith. And that was because he was the most grumpy person anyone had ever known. Oliver had heard men sitting around the stove in winter and in the shade of birches in summer, discussing this, comparing the grumpiness of Mr. Campbell to people they'd known back home, and they could never think of anyone to match the bad temper of the surly blacksmith. Oliver had also listened to the women of Fort William, at a summer picnic, trying to remember when, if ever, one of them had seen a smile on the man's face. No, they decided, he was not a kind man, he had less heart than some animals they'd known – God forgive them for saying so – and he would certainly not do as a husband for the Miss Cottingham at the Post Office. Which was why they'd been discussing Mr. Campbell in the first place.

But everyone had to deal with him: he was the only blacksmith in either of the two towns. So people from the Fort were forced to make the journey to the Landing.

And now there he was: hollering across the street at Oliver. Oliver would have liked to hide! But the blacksmith had come out of his shop and was standing in front of his wide open doorway, waving a thick, flannel-covered arm. In his hand, he held Oliver's snowshoes.

"Come here, Oliver, lad!" he shouted, and so, with a last glance at the open door of the saloon and Miss Darbyshire, Oliver moved in his direction, dragging his boots through the snow.

"Come in," Mr. Campbell commanded, without looking directly at him, and Oliver followed the blacksmith into the cave-like workshop, dark except for two tiny windows in the far corner. "Sit," Mr. Campbell said, and motioned to a long bench. Oliver sat down, glad for the warmth of the stove. In the darkness, his eyes were drawn to the glow of the blacksmith's fire, and the bellows with their wheezing movement. Mr. Campbell handed the snowshoes to him.

"These will be yours then," he said.

Oliver wondered how he had known.

Mr. Campbell returned to the hearth and continued his work on an axe blade, purple with heat. "Don't let your mum catch you taking a peek at Miss Darbyshire's knees," he commanded.

Oliver flushed. He'd been so obvious.

Mr. Campbell was looking across the street, in the direction of the saloon. "Your mum wouldn't call Miss Darbyshire a lady. No one in Fort Willy or Prince would make that mistake. But she's a kind woman, and some people might be mistaken about that." He hesitated before the word "kind," as if it was a word that didn't come easily from his lips.

Oliver had never heard Miss Darbyshire referred to as a kind woman. Perhaps by saying so Mr. Campbell was revealing a small streak of kindness in himself. Oliver didn't answer; he just nodded.

"Your father was in last week, shoeing that horse of yours – what's-his-name?"

"Mac," Oliver muttered.

"Yeah – Mac." Mr. Campbell stared at Oliver, as if he might say something, but then he didn't.

"Father sold him – to Mr. Phillips."

"That a fact? What would Phillips want with a horse like that?"

Mr. Campbell was talking more to himself than he was to Oliver. "Strange thing, it is, Phillips buying up a number of the few horses 'round here."

"He is?"

"He is – your Mac isn't the only one. He bought Mr. Neil's Nellie, and widow Lucas's Trotmore. I wonder what he's up to." Mr. Campbell's voice had lowered until Oliver could hardly hear his mutterings. The blacksmith set his work aside and moved to the stove, wiping his hands on his long leather apron. The tool belts around his waist rattled as he poured steaming coffee out of the cast iron kettle on the stove into a tin mug and slurped a great slurp. Oliver wondered how he could drink it that hot. But perhaps he'd worked so long with his great fire that he was used to such heat.

Then he sat down next to Oliver.

Oliver didn't move, though he would have liked to. Even the warmth of the stove did nothing to make him want to sit next to this crusty human being.

"I hear your father is looking for work. He's had a hard time of it in this place, hasn't he? I'd ask him to help here, but I haven't enough to keep a man properly busy." Mr. Campbell scowled as he spoke, and seemed angry about something.

"He worked at the docks for awhile before the ice, and Mr. Kruger needed help with harvesting cranberries and mending the barn. Father made a harness for his dogs too. He still likes to work with leather," Oliver said.

"Well, it's too bad," said Mr. Campbell. "He comes here expecting to bind books, but nobody in this country reads – at least, nobody makes books." Mr. Campbell's tone was angry.

Oliver wondered what he could be so angry about. He'd had the same angry tone of voice when he'd spoken of Miss Darbyshire's kindness, and how people were mistaken about her.

"Crazy people in these damned towns!" Mr. Campbell threw the last splash of his coffee onto the flames, and the fire hissed and smoked. He stood up to return to his work. His back was turned to Oliver.

"These towns have hated each other for so long, sometimes I think they can't even remember why. It was the railway thing for so long. Before that it was the newspapers. It's always been something. When you're looking for a fight, you'll find it. And they think I'm the grump! Ha!"

Oliver didn't know what to say.

Then that uncanny ability of Mr. Campbell's emerged once again: that ability to know what was not right.

"Fighting is a deadly thing, Oliver, lad. Don't do it, I tell ye!" The blacksmith punctuated his words with a loud clang of steel on steel, and sparks showered from his anvil.

Did Mr. Campbell know about him and Bert? What did he know about Oliver's father and Uncle Will? What didn't he know? Though he was sitting in front of the stove, Oliver shivered.

Mr. Campbell interrupted these thoughts. "I want you to come work for me, boy. I haven't enough decent work for your father, but you can cut wood for my fire and stack it in the corner, and fill my coffee pot, and sort irons. I'll show you where the clinker goes. And I'll pay you. You have school, I know, so you can come on Friday – start tomorrow even – and stay till Saturday. I'll put you up. In the spring, when there's more light, you can go home Friday night." He paused, then said, "I'll see you on Friday then." Clang! went his hammer again, and Oliver knew that he'd not been asked if he'd like to work for this man: he'd been told. Oliver wished that he'd never thought about wanting a job – was that only this morning he'd wished for one? Why?

Well, perhaps this was it. This was the job he'd asked for and, as of the very next day, he would be an employee of Mr. Clifford Campbell, Blacksmith, Prince Arthur's Chief Grump.

Chapter 5

OLIVER'S MOTHER ASSUMED THAT HE'D SPENT THE previous afternoon with Bert, and the following morning she seemed anxious to know how Aunt Emily was. But she waited until after Oliver's father had left the house.

Somehow, the rest of the family knew not to mention Uncle Will and his family in front of Father. When something was bothering Father – as Oliver knew this fight was – he never spoke of it. He seemed to think that by not speaking of it, he could protect his family from the pain or whatever it was that he was feeling. And he also seemed to think that no one else should speak of it either.

So now Mum spoke softly, as if he might hear. "Did Aunt Emily say anything?"

"I didn't go inside the house," Oliver said. He wasn't lying, he told himself. He was evading the truth, but that was different from lying.

"And Bert didn't say anything?"

No, Bert hadn't said a word. Oliver didn't tell his mother that Bert hadn't spoken at all. How could he tell Mum?

"They are our best friends in this place," said Mum. "We need them."

Oliver nodded. He wished he could think of something to say to change the subject. Of course he could tell Mum that he had a job, but for some reason – he wasn't sure why – he hesitated. Maybe because that would mean explaining that no, he hadn't spent time with Bert, or maybe because he wasn't sure about the job itself. What if he really didn't like working for Mr. Campbell? He was certain he wouldn't. But there was the question of money. How much would he make? What would he do with it? He knew what he wanted to do with it.

He wanted to buy Old Mac back from Mr. Phillips.

He watched his Mum. She worked on the other side of the table, with a large pale brown lump of elastic dough. She grasped the outer edges of the dough and pushed them into the centre, again and again and again. She was frowning. She reached into the wooden box for more flour, but the carved scoop she held in her hand came out of the box, empty. She stopped momentarily, pushed her hair back into its knot, and for the first time, looked at Oliver.

"That'll be the end of the flour," was all she said.

How could Oliver think to buy Old Mac back when his family needed flour?

Maybe Mr. Campbell was the grumpiest man in the Landing and the Fort, but he had given Oliver a job. And even though Mr. Campbell hadn't said so, Oliver suddenly realized that he'd given him the job for one reason only: so that Oliver could help out his family. Mr. Campbell hadn't hired help before. Why else would he start now?

But that was an unlikely thing for Mr. Campbell to do. The more Oliver thought about it – the time he'd spent sitting in front of the blacksmith's fire, the offer of a job, Mr. Campbell's strange words about Miss Darbyshire – the more he thought about it, the more like a dream it seemed. Maybe it hadn't really happened. Maybe he'd walk through the blacksmith's door and Mr. Campbell would stare at him, and tell him to leave. Maybe it was a joke. Oliver thought of all the horrible things he'd heard about Mr. Campbell's meanness. It could be a joke.

"Mum?" he asked, standing up from the table and picking up his breakfast plate to wash, "what do you think of Mr. Campbell?"

His mother hesitated. "I don't really know him at all."

"But last summer, at the picnic, I remember

you saying that he was the most miserable person you'd ever met."

"Did I say that? I don't remember."

"Yes – you and Aunt Emily and widow Lucas were discussing whether or not Mr. Campbell should be invited to dinner with Miss Cottingham of the Post Office."

"We were discussing that? You shouldn't listen to our conversations."

Sometimes Oliver wondered about adults. If they discussed things they didn't want you to hear, why did they discuss them where you could?

Friday was always a short day at school. Miss Groom let the students off early, and usually Oliver walked Alberta and Eliza home before setting off to spend the rest of the day, and sometimes the night, in the Landing with Bert.

Mum would have tea steeping in her precious china pot – the pot she'd brought from home, packed so carefully – and hot scones would be warming on the stove. Hannah always waited by the door and pounced on Oliver as he came through it. She was always so disappointed when he left for Bert's. But in the time she had with her big brother home, she would sit next to him, watch him drink his tea, and often he'd read a story to her, or tell her about something that Miss Groom had taught them that day. Eliza would correct him, or recall a detail that he hadn't, and Alberta would make up and sing a noisy chorus about some part of the story. Gavin was so independent. He would sit by the stove and make up his own stories. He didn't care about listening to his brother and sisters. He wanted to go to the whitewashed schoolhouse and hear Miss Groom for himself. "Next year," Mum always said to him, but he couldn't wait.

Once he did follow Oliver and Eliza and Alberta, and no one found him until after they'd sung "God Save the Queen," and then there was a loud hiccough from Gavin, crouched under the coats hung on the back wall. Oliver had had to take him home, and Gavin had grumbled all the way. "Why can't I stay? Why can't I go to school?"

Today, Oliver tried to tell Hannah one of Miss Groom's stories, but his thoughts couldn't keep up with the words, and when Eliza corrected him for the third time – she always noticed mistakes – he told her to take over. He stood up and took his jacket and the snowshoes off the peg.

Mum looked sad. "I hate to see you travelling without Old Mac. I've never worried about you before. It's very cold." She handed Oliver his food sack and hugged him.

"Tell Aunt Emily that I miss her," she said, as she stood at the door watching him leave.

Oliver nodded, then hurried on his way. Mr. Campbell was putting the final shoe on a horse when Oliver arrived. "There we go," he said, and patted the animal's leg. The owner of the horse, a man that Oliver did not recognize, seemed pleased, and reached into a deep pocket in his trousers.

"Here's your pay. Hope you don't mind raw silver. My wife will be happy with your work here. I'm leaving the horse with her while I'm gone on the trail."

Mr. Campbell had been kneeling on the floor, next to the horse. Now his head jerked up. "You're goin', are you? They got you then!"

The man's smile disappeared. "If you must put it that way, yes, they got me. I need a job, Campbell! I'll not be gone long."

"Aye. 'Tis dangerous. Watch your step. Don't slip for an instant, man." Mr. Campbell's head turned. He'd finally caught sight of Oliver standing in the doorway.

The man left abruptly, and the blacksmith watched him from the door. Then he reentered the shop, shaking his head, muttering, angry again. He still hadn't spoken to Oliver.

Oliver wondered what it was that was so dangerous, but he wasn't sure how to ask Mr. Campbell. After all, he wasn't even sure if he had this job. But Mr. Campbell answered that question in short order.

"The axe is there. Split the logs 'round the corner. First have some coffee with me, Oliver."

Oliver hadn't had coffee before. Father said he could when he was thirteen, next year. Mr. Campbell poured the dark liquid from the pot on the stove. It was bitter, but warmed Oliver after his walk. Now that one question was answered, and he really did have a job, he felt braver about asking the other.

"What is it that's dangerous?"

Mr. Campbell looked over the rim of his heavy mug. "That'll be the dynamite – the nitroglycerin. It looks like molasses, and one drop will blow off a man's leg. Jack there, he's been hired to carry it east, up around the lake a bit."

Oliver had heard about dynamite. It was used to blow open the rocks and mountains of this strange and wild land that his family had come to. Sometimes, it seemed that this country did not want tracks laid over it, nor people to cross it. The land itself defied roads and railway tracks, and paths could be cleared only with horrible and violent means.

"Nitroglycerin works best to clear the rocks. But it's difficult to move." Mr. Campbell didn't seem to be able to stop shaking his head. He pulled a silver flask from inside his shirt, opened it with one hand, and poured a bit of amber liquid into his coffee. He didn't offer any to Oliver. Oliver sipped more coffee. He was getting used to the bitterness. Maybe someday he'd even like it.

Mr. Campbell continued. "Can't carry the stuff on horseback – the horses move too much. Can't possibly move it by train. No – it's only men that can move it. And sometimes they jostle it too much, and then that's it." He made a sound of something blowing up, and waved the flask in the air, a shot of silver. "Dozens of men at a time. And does anyone care?" Mr. Campbell scowled. "No! They just hire more – and there's always more – more and more men looking for work, with hungry families." He poured another splash from the flask, drank it from the mug, and stood up. "Time to chop wood,Oliver, lad!"

Oliver chopped wood until well after dinner time and piled it in the corner of the shop. Then he refilled the coffee pot with water for the next day, and swept the dirt floor, first shovelling the horse manure that one of the "customers" of the day had left behind.

Mr. Campbell didn't speak to him again until his work was done, and then all he said was, "Follow me, lad." He led him to a door that Oliver hadn't noticed before. The door opened into Mr. Campbell's home, which was small, just one room, and like Oliver's home, had a loft. Only Mr. Campbell's loft was just big enough for one feather tick mattress. He told Oliver he could sleep in the main room on the wooden bench against the wall. There was a quilt folded over the back of the bench, and Mr. Campbell had already put a fluffy pillow on one end. Oliver noted the pillow with some surprise. Mr. Campbell didn't seem like the kind of person who had fluffy pillows.

"Beans are on the menu tonight," said Oliver's new boss, and he disappeared out the door that led to the street. He was gone for a few minutes, then he returned with a bean crock in his gloved hands. He set it quickly on the stove, removed his gloves, and rubbed his hands. "It's hot, that pot is." He reached behind him to close the door.

Oliver wondered where he'd gotten the crock from.

"Outside – it's been under the snow since yesterday morning. Ha!" Mr. Campbell opened the lid and was obviously pleased. "This is the way my mother made them. Dig a hole in the snow, set a fire in it – I use slow-burning saw-dust – put your bean crock there and bury it. Come back, and it's better than a crock of gold, though you can't say that too loudly in a mining town!"

Oliver moved closer and took a sniff of the beans, light brown, still bubbling with maple syrup and salt pork. He began to salivate. He hadn't realized how hungry he was.

Mr. Campbell filled two tin plates with the beans and set them on the table.

"My mother came to this place in the 'thirties. She loved it here. Not like some who run back home with their tail between their legs. She really loved it. She never could understand why the people here fought. Why there had to be so much strife between towns. Mostly, she ignored the fighting and made friends with Prince people and with people from Fort Willy. She adapted her ways to this cold place, and she loved it."

Oliver had lost count of how many times Mr. Campbell had said that his mother loved it here, but he didn't interrupt. Mr. Campbell's voice was usually so gruff and angry, but now that same gruffness had a comforting quality, and Oliver didn't listen so much to the man's words, as to the bass rumblings. He could feel himself becoming sleepy from all the work he'd done earlier, and though he didn't usually like warm milk, he didn't protest at all when Mr. Campbell stirred some for him on the stove and handed him a full mug. Then the blacksmith climbed the ladder to the loft and left Oliver with the light of a single candle. He didn't say anything like "good night." He just nodded, and Oliver curled up on the wide bench, pulled the faded quilt over himself, set the empty mug aside, and blew out the candle.

Chapter 6

EARLY SATURDAY MORNING OLIVER AWOKE TO THE sound of knuckles on wood, and without thinking, stood up and wrapped the quilt around himself. He went to the door and opened it as if it were his own. He was not yet awake.

Bert stood outside. He stared at Oliver, and Oliver stared back, and neither said a word.

Up in the loft, Mr. Campbell called, "Who's there?"

Oliver opened his mouth to answer, but Bert hollered first. "I am sir! Bert here. But I'll be going." He turned to leave, back through the snow.

Oliver called, "Bert!" His cousin didn't turn, but he did stop and look over his shoulder.

"I thought you were never going to speak to me again," Bert said. Then he did turn around and walk away.

Oliver kicked into the snow that was banked to the side of the door. The snow was ice-hard underneath a thin topping of new flakes, and his toes smashed against it. That Bert! He was so stubborn. He wouldn't even give Oliver half a chance to say anything. Well, Oliver could be stubborn too. He could be even more stubborn....

"He's gone, is he?" There was a thump as Mr. Campbell landed on the floor. He'd jumped down from halfway up the ladder. "I wanted to see Bert this morning. I needed to order something from his father's store."

"Did you ask him to come here?" Oliver asked.

"Aye. I thought with you here, he'd come in and chat for a bit." Mr. Campbell squinted his eyes at Oliver. "You've had a wee falling out, have you?"

Oliver didn't say anything. He had an idea that somehow Mr. Campbell already knew the answer to that question – with all his talk about fighting!

Mr. Campbell set about brewing coffee and as he worked, Oliver watched his face. First his brows lowered and great lines filled his forehead, and slowly his mouth pulled back at the corners, his upper lip raised in a sneer, so that, by the time he'd finished with the coffee, his face had his characteristic miserable look. Oliver wondered if it was always this way with Mr. Campbell. It occurred to Oliver that Mr.

Campbell wore his grumpiness just as some people did their clothes. But if Oliver were to share this thought with anyone, no one would believe him. He wasn't even sure of it himself. He had a lingering feeling that at an unexpected moment, Mr. Campbell would turn suddenly and snarl at him. Instead he tried to remember what the man had looked like the evening before as he'd warmed milk on the stove and handed a mug of it to Oliver.

"Here's coffee, and milk for your oatmeal." Mr. Campbell pushed the milk across the rough table top. Then he set an envelope beside Oliver's bowl. "Bring the envelope with you next week," he added gruffly.

This was Oliver's pay. He wanted to reach out, grab the crumpled envelope, and stuff it into the pocket in his shirt, but he didn't.

"I won't need you today at all, lad. You can be going as soon as you've finished up at the table." Mr. Campbell went out through the door into the blacksmithing shop.

Oliver swallowed the last of the coffee, even though it burned his throat, and pulled his jacket on. He wrapped his muffler over his head and around his neck once he was outside. And opened the envelope before he put on the mitts he'd borrowed from Eliza.

Ten cents!

His own money. For a split second, he could

almost hear the sound of Old Mac's hooves at his side, feel the snort of steamy horse-breath. Old Mac would be his again.

Then Oliver thought of his mother and the empty flour bin.

But it would be so easy to work for Mr. Campbell and earn enough money to pay back Mr. Phillips. Especially now that he and Bert, and Uncle Will and Father were all at odds. Oliver's parents would assume that he spent Friday nights at Bert's. They wouldn't have to know until Oliver arrived at the house one morning on the back of Old Mac. Then they'd be so surprised and happy to see the horse, that they wouldn't think to chastise him. Or by then Father would have a job, and they would understand this decision of Oliver's.

But what about Mum's flour bin? How could Oliver keep this ten cents? Even ten cents would buy some flour.

He trudged home on his snowshoes, moved slowly, though he knew he'd be late for Saturday tea. As always, he passed the buildings of the Powder Company, but this time he paused. So this was where the nitroglycerin was made. He moved on still pondering, his fingers clutching the coin in his pocket. When he opened the door of his home he almost stumbled over the crock of milk, the potatoes, and the sack of flour just inside the doorway.

Father was sitting in his place at the table.

"We've been waiting for you," Father said, and he stood up from the table. "I have an announcement to make. I have a job."

At the word "job," Mum started up from the table, but she fell back to her seat, with a strange look on her face. The rest of the family was quiet.

Eliza and Alberta were watching their mother's face. Gavin stopped chewing the thick piece of bread that he'd stuffed into his mouth. Hannah didn't notice anything amiss. She continued tugging on her mother's skirt, hoping for attention, now that the room was finally silent.

Oliver's father waved his hands in the air. "Now, now," he said, "No long faces! It's time for happiness. The Tate family has flour once again, and I have a job."

"What job?" asked Mum quietly.

"A fine job, Beth, a fine job," he answered.

"Where?" she insisted.

"I'll have to go away for a while, but it won't be long."

"When do you leave?"

"Tomorrow morning." Father spoke these words very quietly. And then quickly said, "They've given me an advance on my earnings – five dollars! Wasn't that good of them?"

"They gave you an advance even before you've worked a day?" Mum seemed impressed with this. She even forgot that Father hadn't said what the job was.

Father took some coins out of the pocket in his trousers and handed them to Mum. "Here is what's left. You might need it. When I get back, I'll have more."

Oliver only half listened to this conversation. He once again felt the ten cents in his own pocket. It was his! His own for certain now. He didn't need to give it to his father. The family would be fine – Father had a job again and soon Old Mac would be home where he belonged.

Father was gone before the sun had raised its head. Oliver awoke early too and lay under his quilt listening to the rumble and murmur of his parents, and then a brief moment of stillness that he knew was a hug, before the door closed behind his father. There was another moment before the clatter of Mum taking dishes from shelves for the breakfast table. And that moment of silence ended with a loud sniffle, then the sound of a blown nose.

Oliver wanted to get up, but if Mum was having a bit of a cry, perhaps she wanted to be alone. He'd wait a while, he decided. Sometimes it seemed that he hadn't really known his parents until the family had had to be cramped into their alloted space on the ship from

Liverpool. In the weeks crossing the Atlantic Ocean he'd come to know the rhythmic snoring of his father, the subtle fluctuations of mood in his mother – things he'd never noticed back home, when walls had separated them at night, and school and city bustle had separated them during the day. But on the ship, with its stacked and close bunks, and elbow-bumping benches at mealtimes, and now in the quietness of this over-sized country, he'd come to know his family better than ever before. Now he knew to give Mum a moment to herself.

But the clatter of dishes overtook the silence. Oliver could see Eliza's red-brown head turn as she moved, waking up. She must have struck her sister with an elbow because Alberta jumped suddenly in her sleep and turned over once, taking most of the quilts with her. Oliver thought it was a good time to leave the loft – before the two began a quilt tussle or worse, a pillow war. Last time that happened all the children, even Hannah, had had to spend the morning cleaning the bits of goose down that clung to everything in the loft.

Mum was sipping tea and looking out the one small front window. Oliver noticed that she'd put an old plate on the mantel in the place left empty by the books.

He took a wide mug without handles from the open shelf and, hoping Mum wouldn't see, filled it with the coffee that his father had left behind. He was getting used to the bitter taste of the dark, heavy liquid. He felt rather grown up this morning, with his coffee in hand, his ten cents still in his pocket, and his father away.

Mum broke his thoughts. "Your father won't be too long. I hope he'll be safe." She continued to stare out the window as she spoke. She didn't look at Oliver. Oliver had a sudden desperate feeling: the same feeling he'd had the afternoon before when his father announced he had a job.

"Did he tell you about the work he'll be doing?" he asked.

Mum frowned. "Not really – just that he must make a trip east."

A trip east! That sounded familiar. That was the same direction that Jack, Mr. Campbell's customer, was going! Oliver could hear Mr. Campbell's voice saying, "'Tis dangerous – watch your step – don't slip for an instant, man."

Nitroglycerin. Horses couldn't carry it, railway cars couldn't carry it. Only men could carry it. Men with hungry families. That's what Mr. Campbell had said. Men like Oliver's father.

Coffee splashed over the wall as Oliver dropped his mug.

"Oliver!" His mother leaped up from her chair. "Oliver – what is it?"

He threw his jacket on, and grabbed his snowshoes. "I've got to stop him, Mum. He can't go...."

"What are you talking about?" Mum's question followed him, but he didn't answer as he struggled with his snowshoes to the Krugers' front gate. He pushed his way towards their door.

Maybe Mr. Kruger would lend him his horse.

Then Oliver heard bells behind him and turned around. Mr. Kruger was bringing 'round the cutter from the barn. Oliver noticed the farmer's fancy black hat. Of course – it was Sunday – he was on his way to church.

Mr. Kruger left the horse prancing in one place in the snow as he passed by on his way into the house. "Just have to get the Missus – be with you in a minute, Oliver." Mr. Kruger disappeared into the house even as Oliver opened his mouth to speak.

The door closed behind the man. Oliver stared after him for a long minute, then towards the horse and cutter. Those sharp runners could cut a path to town so quickly. He looked again at the closed door. And back at the horse. Maybe Mr. Kruger wouldn't mind missing church, just once.

Oliver raced over, and leapt into the cutter. There was a bearskin on the seat, and he pulled it over his knees. Mr. Kruger, followed by his wife, came out the door just as he sped away.

"Oliver! Come back – where are you going? What do you think you are doing?"

"I have to find my father! I'll be back. I will!" Oliver called over his shoulder. He'd never ridden so quickly. The wind seemed to take the breath right out of his mouth. His nostrils burned. He had to almost close his eyes. And this horse knew where she was supposed to be going, so Oliver had to work to keep her from heading in the direction of the church.

Anyone leaving on a nitroglycerin trek would be leaving from the Ontario Powder Company.

Then he saw the factory buildings in the distance, and when he neared, all was still. No one was working on Sunday, and if a group of men had set out earlier, there was no immediate sign of them. Oliver jumped out of the cutter, and tied the horse to a nearby birch. He approached the office building, and there, by the side door was an area where the snow was scuffled and flattened. A short distance away, a great number of footprints formed an orderly trail. Oliver couldn't discern his father's footprints from the others, but he knew they must be there. He knocked heavily on the door. No one answered. He pounded with his hands together in a fist, striking at the wood with his lower arms. No one answered. He turned with his back to the door and slipped to a sitting position on the hard-packed snow step and held his head in his hands. His mother's words came back to him – "this is a wretched and wild place."

Oliver stood suddenly and kicked at the office door, which barely moved for his effort, then he turned and walked back to where Belle stood by the birch. She was sweating. He'd run her too hard, and he should have rubbed her down before leaving her standing in the cold. Perhaps he should press on after his father, but it was probably too late. He could ask Mr. Campbell for help. Mr. Campbell had told him about the nitroglycerin; he might know more.

He'd best walk the horse – keep her warm, he thought – and he led her by the halter, towards the Landing. Every step delayed having to face the Krugers. How would he tell them why he'd run off with Belle and their sled? And he didn't want to have to tell Mum where Father had gone and what his job was.

Why hadn't Father told her himself? Again, Oliver was angry with him. His father never told the family anything. Not about this job, not about the fight with Uncle Will, not even about this country he'd brought them to. All he'd said about this place was that it was a "beautiful land of opportunity." Bah! thought Oliver. Sure his father'd found a job: a job he might never return home from. Did he think he could protect his family by not telling them anything? If he did, he was wrong. Silence didn't help.

But angry as he was, when he thought of his father, he felt his stomach turn. He was afraid, and his fear curled up and settled itself in him. He knew it would stay until his father returned home.

"Uncle Will!" Oliver said his uncle's name before he could stop himself. His uncle was striding down the middle of Arthur Street, moving in Oliver's direction. He had a grim expression on his face, but that changed as he heard Oliver's call and looked up.

"Did you walk out of church again?" Oliver asked. Uncle Will was well known for leaving halfway through the sermon. It was hardly scandalous anymore, he'd done it so often – usually when the weather was warm and fishing in the lake just too inviting. Oliver wondered why he'd left this cold winter day.

Uncle Will seemed pleased with himself. "I did! I don't like that man, the Reverend, but you know how it is; Aunt Emily makes me go. Says she'll be lonely in heaven without me if I don't."

Oliver felt strange talking with his uncle as if nothing had happened.

Uncle Will stooped and peered at him.

"Why haven't you been around, Oliver? The fight your father and I had is nothing between you and Bert."

So he didn't know then.

"Or is it?" asked Uncle Will.

"Might be, sir," Oliver admitted.

"I'm sorry to hear that," said Uncle Will, and

he did look sad. "I don't know when your father and I will patch things up," he said next, but to Oliver's ears it sounded as if he'd said, "I don't know *if* we'll patch things up," and the word "stubborn" came into Oliver's mind, like an echo. Stubborn, stubborn, stubborn – your father is stubborn.

Maybe Uncle Will was the stubborn one. Maybe Bert was. Maybe Oliver was. But Oliver had a reason to be so. He did have a reason....

Uncle Will was looking at Belle. "I think you ought to keep that animal moving," he said. "And I'll be going – I have work to do."

Work? On Sunday? That was going too far, even for Uncle Will.

Uncle Will was shaking his head. "Scrawny Joe has left me – gone to new country opening up west. Wants to try farming the soil there. I told him it's not good, but he must go and see for himself. So I'm on my own ... although maybe it's just as well. He made a mistake with his ordering, and now I'm left with a shipment of sheets of glass. It came yesterday, and fills the entire store – no room to move. And your aunt's not happy; I've used every blessed blanket and quilt we own to wrap it all, to keep it from breaking. We're going to be freezing in our nightshirts! Now I have to make room for it, or I won't be able to open tomorrow."

Joe'd been at the store since before Uncle Will opened. In fact, most of Will's customers had come because they knew and trusted Joe. Many times Bert and Oliver had listened to Scrawny Joe's stories about the West. Joe still called it "Rupert's Land," and he had many fantastic tales to tell. Oliver couldn't imagine the store without Scrawny Joe.

Things were changing so quickly. Why was it that as soon as you were no longer speaking to someone, big changes happened in both your lives, changes so great that you ended up feeling even further from that person?

Oliver tightened his hold on Belle's halter. "Tell Aunt Emily that Mum says 'hello.'" At least he could deliver Mum's greetings.

Uncle Will nodded and reached out to rub Belle's nose.

"Isn't this Kruger's animal? Where's Old Mac?"

"Father sold him," Oliver answered softly.

"Sold him?" Uncle Will's face twisted. "Sold him? First his books, now Old Mac. What else will he sell?" Uncle Will was muttering as he walked away. He didn't even say goodbye.

So he knew about the books.

Oliver watched him until he unlocked the front door of the store and disappeared inside. Then Oliver climbed into the cutter and lightly slapped Belle with the reins. He turned her homeward and she began to trot down the middle of the roadway. Oliver passed a saloon. Today – Sunday – the doors were closed, but the sound of music could be heard, and it wasn't the church organ. In this town there was always music and dance and something to drink. Oliver could imagine what his father would have to say about that.

Church service would soon be over, and Oliver didn't want to run into Bert. Besides, he had to get Belle back to Mr. Kruger. He didn't know what he was going to tell the farmer. He supposed that the truth would probably be the best, but there'd be so much to explain then. Still, there'd be even more to explain if he didn't tell the truth.

It was noon, and the bell of St. Andrew's church began to toll over the country between the two towns. Oliver loved the hollow-sounding boom of the bell. It was something he looked forward to each Sunday. He could hear that bell even when he was at home.

Of course, the bell did have another purpose besides calling the congregation to worship. It was also a warning bell; if anything went wrong, someone would ring it. But in all the time that Oliver had lived in the Fort, he'd never heard that sound except on Sunday mornings.

Now the clanging followed Oliver, and an idea occurred to him. He finally let go of the reins, gave Belle her head, and sat back warming his hands under the bearskin. The reins danced over the rounded front of the cutter as Belle turned in the direction of the Krugers' church.

The small congregation was beginning to leave through the double doors. Belle brought Oliver and the cutter to a stop several feet from the lowest step. Reverend Birney stood at the door, bidding people good day.

"You're a bit late!" he called to Oliver, but he smiled and waved as he spoke.

The Krugers came outside just then. Mrs. Kruger headed straight for the opening at the side of the cutter.

"See, Herman? I told you he'd fetch us home." She climbed in and smiled broadly at Oliver – who felt guilty and was not at all sure he deserved her trust.

Mr. Kruger glared at Oliver before he swung himself into his seat. "Have you lost your mind, boy? Disappearing with a sleigh and horse that is no property of yours? Some people would call it stealing!"

"I had to borrow it, sir," began Oliver.

"Oh! Borrowing is what you call it!" Mr. Kruger seemed to be growing more angry.

His wife spoke up. "I'm sure Oliver had a good reason – didn't you, Oliver?"

Oliver nodded. "I had to go after my father. I think he's taken a job carrying nitroglycerin."

Mrs. Kruger put a hand to her mouth and made a sound like a hiccough.

Mr. Kruger glanced over at her, then at Oliver. Then he looked straight ahead at the rump of

Belle, jogging along the road. They were almost at the farm. "You could have told me," he said. "I would have come with you." He still sounded angry.

"I'm very sorry, Mr. Kruger. I didn't want to make you angry."

Mr. Kruger turned quickly to Oliver, and Oliver realized then that he wasn't angry. He was still frowning, but now it was a worried frown. "I don't suppose you found your father?" he said.

"No, sir."

At the farm Belle stopped by the gate, and Mr. Kruger climbed out and went around the cutter to help his wife out. He put out his arm for Oliver to take hold of as he jumped out.

"Oliver," said Mr. Kruger, "I'm sorry we didn't have any more work for your father here on the farm."

Oliver shook his hand. "It's not your fault, Mr. Kruger. There's not much to be done in winter."

"Let me know if there's anything I can do," Mr. Kruger said.

"Thank you. I'll take Belle to the barn now."

"That would be good of you." Mr. Kruger began to walk away, but he turned back. "If you see Pepper in there, say hello for me. She seems to like hiding out in the barn."

Pepper was one of the Krugers' sleddogs, a middle-aged mutt with a friendly face. In summer, she often followed Hannah, pulling on her skirt if she went too close to the river.

Oliver took Belle to the barn door, unharnessed her from the cutter, led her inside, and began to rub her down thoroughly. There was Pepper, in a dark corner sleeping in the hay, but she sat up as Oliver entered, and he paused a moment to scratch behind her ears.

Then he dragged the cutter to the side shed and left for home.

Eliza and Alberta were standing by the big maple tree waiting for him. Neither had enough clothes on for the cold, and they'd obviously been there for a while.

"Where did you run off to, Oliver?" asked Eliza. "You frightened Mum."

"Mum's going mad," said Alberta flatly. Eliza pushed her elbow into Alberta's ribs.

"She's not going *mad*!" Eliza said.

"Well, she did drop her teapot." Alberta sounded as if her mind was quite made up about her mother's madness. And at the same time, it didn't seem to bother her one bit. For a moment, Oliver wished he was as young as she was.

"The teapot's in a hundred pieces now," said Eliza. "What are you going to do, Oliver?"

Eliza's question made Oliver feel suddenly old and tired.

"I don't know," he answered.

"Did she really drop her teapot?" It seemed such a strange question. Such an unimportant question. With such an important answer.

Eliza paused. "No – she threw it."

Chapter 7

WHEN OLIVER HEARD THAT, HE GRABBED A HAND of each sister and pulled them towards the cabin. This was not good. Sure Mum could have her low points, but usually she was like waves on a small lake: not much distance between the high points and the low ones. She'd never lost her temper enough to do something like this. Maybe she did have some idea of where Father had gone after all.

Mum was sitting, with her head on her arms on the table, her face hidden, when they walked through the door. Oliver guessed that she'd probably been in that position for a long time. Gavin was sitting quietly in his place by the stove, and for once he had no food in his mouth. Even Hannah was unusually quiet. She didn't bounce up, like she always did when she saw Oliver, but she did go directly to him, and wrested his hand away from Eliza's. Her eyes, always adoring, had something new in them. Something desperate, pleading with Oliver to do something, to make it all right.

"Mum?" began Oliver tentatively. For a split second he wondered how he was going to tell her about Father's job. Best deal with the teapot first.

"What happened, Mum?"

Mum didn't raise her head. "My teapot fell," she said.

"Sideways," added Alberta. She pointed to the stain on the wall. There were still shards of china on the floor under the spot.

Mum finally raised her head. Her eyelids were puffy and red.

"Yes," she agreed, "it fell sideways." And a funny little smile tried to fasten itself to the corners of her mouth but gave up, and Mum began to cry instead.

"Where did you go?" she asked.

"The Powder Company," he said. "Father wasn't there," he added. He could feel Hannah staring at him, and he knew that she wouldn't understand his next words, but she might be able to guess at their meaning, so he made his voice light. "I think he's carrying nitroglycerin for the company."

Mum looked at him and nodded. Just the smallest of nods, but Oliver knew that she'd already known or guessed. Hannah let go of

Oliver's hand and moved to stand next to Mum. Softly she patted her arm. Oliver wrapped his arms around Mum's shoulders.

Gavin must have decided that he'd had about enough of tears. It was time to eat, he must have figured, and reached for the bread that Mum always kept on the table, under a cloth. He put some in his mouth, and didn't speak until after he'd chewed and swallowed noisily.

"Yeah," he said decisively. "The teapot fell sideways."

Everyone in the room stared at him, and Mum started to laugh. Oliver was the last to join in the laughter, but when he did, his was the loudest.

The weather was wild that week, and there was no reason to go to the Landing, so Oliver spent time with his Mum and sisters and brother, much to Hannah's delight. Oliver told her every story he'd ever heard or read, and he and Mum didn't once mention Father or the nitroglycerin trek.

They played euchre every night after dinner when it was dark and the wind caught on the rough corners of the cabin, and when Mum wasn't playing with them, she sat in the rocking chair and stared out the window. Twice Oliver found her there, when the children were in the loft and it was late.

"I'd like to see Emily," she said once, and the fear that had settled in Oliver's belly jumped and turned several times before settling down again to its usual position.

He couldn't bring himself to say anything about Uncle Will or Bert. Mum had enough on her mind.

Oliver wished that there was something he could do, but Father was somewhere out there and Oliver could only wait for his return.

Friday, Oliver trudged through the snow to Mr. Campbell's. A part of him dreaded seeing the man; he wondered how much the blacksmith knew about his family. Another part of him, though, looked forward to being away from home, where Mum's worried face watched his anxiously.

It was almost dark when he arrived; the trip had taken him longer than usual, and the shop was in complete darkness. Even the fire was out. Oliver went around to the door of Mr. Campbell's home and knocked. Mr. Campbell opened the door immediately, came outside and closed it behind him. He was wearing clean trousers, a coat, muffler, and hat, and had had his usually scruffy beard trimmed.

"I've been waiting for you, Oliver. What a time you've taken!" He removed his hat, felt inside it, punched the crown into a rounded shape he seemed to find more to his approval, and clapped it back on his head.

"Come – we're going to dinner." He strode across the street, leaving Oliver to follow. Oliver hurried after him, three steps to Mr. Campbell's one.

Dinner! He hadn't been out to dinner since before his family moved to Fort William.

But they were passing the Queen's Hotel. Oliver continued after Mr. Campbell, down the street and to the left.

"Wait here," commanded Mr. Campbell, and he disappeared.

Oliver recognized the house. He'd stood outside this place once before. It was where Miss Darbyshire lived.

He could only nod at her when she came out, holding Mr. Campbell's arm to keep from sliding down the slippery front steps.

"Hello, Master Oliver," she said, and smiled gently.

Master Oliver! No one had ever called him that! But he rather liked it.

What would Mum say? Probably little compared to what his father would. Imagine: Oliver Tate going to dinner with Miss Darbyshire and the Prince Arthur Grump.

Inside the Queen's Hotel was warmth and wonderful smells – roasting chicken and venison – and fire crackling in open hearths at either end of the main room. There was the subdued hum of many voices, a sound that Oliver hadn't heard since back home. Of course that would change as the dinner hour became evening, and people began their end-of-week revelry.

Did he imagine it, or was there a moment when some of the guests turned to stare as the three of them entered?

Mr. Campbell looked among the tables near the entrance and the front windows, hoping to find an empty one, but Miss Darbyshire took his elbow and steered him towards the back corner, near the open and wide kitchen door.

"I don't want to sit here, Fiona Darbyshire! It's loud and there are too many people walking by," Mr. Campbell said.

"Well, the three of us can't sit in the front. There are too many people walking by there too," she said.

"That's different," he said, and the lines of his mask seemed to settle deeper into his face.

"Yes – it is different. If we sit in the front, then tomorrow some busybody will be telling Oliver's mother that he was seen having dinner with that saloon dancer. If we sit by the kitchen, she won't hear about it for at least a week!"

"Aye," growled the blacksmith, and he pulled a chair out for Miss Darbyshire to sit down.

Oliver was surprised to hear her speak about herself as she did. After they ordered their meal, and as they waited, Miss Darbyshire answered those who greeted her, and said "How are you" to the people she knew and saw. Mr. Campbell only nodded at men who nodded first at him.

At their table, she was the one who talked the most. Mr. Campbell continued to growl "aye" every so often, and Oliver answered her questions because he couldn't think of any of his own. That is, he could think of things he would have liked to ask her, but they probably weren't polite, so he didn't.

"Tell me about school," she said.

So Oliver told her about Miss Groom, and about Big Kate with her mismatched boots, and Olav who used his eye patch as a sling-shot when anyone teased him about it. He told her about Miss Groom's work on *The Perambulator*, the Fort William newspaper that she'd put together with Mr. McKellar. And he told her about Gavin, and how badly he wanted to start school.

"You're so fortunate," Miss Darbyshire said. "I had to leave school when I was nine." She waved her fork at Mr. Campbell. "He's teaching me more about reading."

"Aye." Mr. Campbell worked at his venison with a dull kitchen knife.

"Someday I'm going to work for a newspaper too!" said Miss Darbyshire.

All this time, Oliver had had a lingering image of this woman's knees; suddenly he saw her with a pencil behind her ear, working at one of the desks in the office of the Landing's *Sentinel.* He even imagined her in trousers! He had to shake his head in order to see the woman in front of him again.

"I think you'll do very well on the newspaper," he said grandly. It was the first time that evening he'd offered his own opinion.

"I'm happy you think so, Master Oliver!" She smiled at him, and seemed pleased.

Oliver glanced at Mr. Campbell, and saw a change in his eyes. He was looking towards the door. Oliver followed his gaze. Uncle Will, Aunt Emily, and Bert were standing there, looking for a table. Aunt Emily caught sight of Oliver first and waved. Then she saw who he was with, and looked confused, as if she'd mistaken his identity; that couldn't be her nephew sitting with two of the most infamous people of the Landing. Uncle Will waved, saluted Mr. Campbell, gave a half bow in Miss Darbyshire's direction. Bert just turned away.

"Isn't that your cousin?" asked Miss Darbyshire. "I remember seeing you two boys out my window once."

She didn't seem angry – maybe even slightly

amused. Just the same, Oliver was glad when Mr. Campbell spoke up.

"The two of 'em have had a falling out," he said gruffly.

"That's too bad," she said softly. "A body needs all the friends he can get in a place like this."

She put a hand towards him and patted his arm. "You ought to fix things up, Master Oliver, and soon, before you lose some pieces and can't fix it."

Mr. Campbell finally sawed through the venison. He lifted it halfway to his mouth. "You should go talk to him." He jerked his head toward Bert and wiped the corner of his mouth where he was noticeably salivating.

"Go, boy!" he urged, his voice strong. He grabbed Oliver's jacket from the back of his chair and held it out.

Oliver pushed his chair back, took the jacket, and stumbled in Bert's direction, feeling as if Mr. Campbell was pushing him forward, feeling as if Miss Darbyshire was guiding his arm. He didn't want to be doing this; he had his pride. But there he was moving closer ... closer....

"Bert?" He was standing in front of him now.

Uncle Will spoke, and sounded just like the blacksmith. "Go, Bert. Talk with your cousin."

Bert stood up, and reached for his coat. "Let's go outside," he said, and led the way.

Chapter 8

OUTSIDE THE COLD WAS MORE INTENSE THAN IT had been when Oliver had gone into the hotel. Bert walked ahead and didn't turn to face Oliver until they were halfway down the street. Then he turned suddenly.

"Am I supposed to say I'm sorry?" he asked. "Why don't you say it first?"

"Why should I?"

Bert stuck his hands in his pockets. He waited for Oliver to speak, which he finally did.

"Why are we doing this?" He began to walk back to the hotel. "This is ridiculous. We are fighting about someone else's fight – it's not even our fight. It's theirs. It has nothing to do with us."

"Sure it does – they're our fathers."

"And? It's their fight."

"Well, it might not affect you, Oliver, but it does affect me!"

"It doesn't have to," said Oliver. He felt that the two of them were not changing the situation at all. They were just standing in the cold, shouting at each other again. He would have been better off to have kept his promise and not said anything at all.

"Well, it does affect me," Bert said.

"How?"

Bert finally stepped forward and stood directly in front of Oliver. "My pa spends every minute of his time in that store since Scrawny Joe left. I hardly ever see him, and when I do, he's scribbling figures on a slate, trying to find if the business is going to work out. Late at night, and on Sunday, he's unpacking things. The other night I heard noises like an earthquake. I went downstairs to the store, and there he was, moving shelves, rearranging the place ... if your father had taken Joe's place like he should have, this wouldn't be happening."

Oliver wasn't sure he'd heard those last words of Bert's.

"What about my father taking Joe's place?"

Bert leaned even closer. "Don't you know? That's what the fight was about – my pa asked your father if he'd like to work in the store. Your father turned him down. Something about he's too good for the Landing; he has to keep his family in Fort William."

Oliver didn't feel the cold any more. "That's

not the truth! He would've told me if your pa offered him a job; he would've taken it!" Oliver wasn't at all certain that his father would have told him such a thing, but he couldn't back down.

"The fight must have been about something else," he said. "Something your pa isn't telling you. Maybe it was about the books again."

"Pa tells me everything. And the books were just the beginning. Your father brought them to the store to sell." Bert's eyes were bright.

So it was the truth then.

"Bah!" said Oliver. It was all he could think of to say. Then he walked into the hotel.

Mr. Campbell and Miss Darbyshire were quiet as he sat down. They seemed to sense that it had not gone well. After several minutes, Mr. Campbell could keep still no longer and cleared his throat with what Oliver had come to recognize as his "I-am-going-to-make-a-speech" cough-snort.

But first he had a question for Oliver.

"Is your anger still alive and well fed?"

Oliver wasn't sure he liked Mr. Campbell's question, but the blacksmith continued.

"So? Why does it live on?" Mr. Campbell was almost growling.

Miss Darbyshire rested her hand gently on his wrist and tugged on his cuff, a small motion to make him stop. But he didn't.

Oliver had finally caught some of Mr. Campbell's foul mood and now he spoke. "Seems my father had a job offer, but Prince Arthur's Landing isn't good enough for him." As soon as the words were out of his mouth, he regretted them.

He knew that Bert had been telling the truth. Oliver knew because he knew his father, and he could imagine how it might have gone.

How had it begun? With Father saying he needed to sell his books? Uncle Will refusing to sell them? Uncle Will telling Oliver's father that Scrawny Joe had left the store, and he needed help?

Oliver could imagine his uncle, all those wrinkles creasing across his face. "John," he'd say, and he'd put his hand on Father's arm, and Father'd pull away; he hated it when anyone felt pity for him. "Come work with me," Uncle Will would say, and he'd say something about family helping family.

Then Oliver's father would say something about a man standing on his own two feet – that was something he said often. Then he would bring up the town – how he didn't want to bring his family to the Landing, it being the kind of place it was, and all.

And Uncle Will would stand up straight – he always stood up for his town – and he'd have asked, "*What* kind of place do you mean?"

And Father would talk about the saloons and the willing-to-gamble miners.

Maybe Uncle Will would try to calm him down by reminding him that his family lived there. Or maybe Uncle Will would make Father more upset by reminding him of how badly he needed work. That was one thing that Oliver's father didn't want to hear.

Maybe Father would turn to stomp out the door, and Uncle Will would grab his arm to keep him from leaving. Maybe that was how Father blackened Uncle Will's eye. Or had Uncle Will hit him first?

Oh, how could it have become so ugly!

Oliver tried to crumple the scene in his own head, but it wasn't easy. He felt so angry with his father. If his father had taken the job, then he, Oliver, wouldn't have to be worrying about him now as he cut into his cold roast turkey and soggy baked apple.

Mr. Campbell reached over and, not unkindly, shoved Oliver's food aside. "Have a few oysters," he said, and pulled his own plate closer. "So – your father thinks Fort Willy is the place to be, does he?" Mr. Campbell ended with a "Ha!" and popped a squishy oyster into his mouth. Oliver did likewise.

Miss Darbyshire looked at him sharply. "Clifford Campbell – you watch your tongue!"

He ignored her and chewed on. "Well! He

does – and I've news for him – some of which he'll find in the *Sentinel* and some of which he won't." Mr. Campbell leaned forward and watched Oliver as he spoke. "But let me tell you – Fort Willy is not the place he believes it to be." He paused and looked at Miss Darbyshire. "And neither is the Landing."

Oliver wasn't sure what Mr. Campbell was trying to tell him, but somehow he knew that whatever the blacksmith was about to say had a great deal in common with those conversations that his father always tried to avoid. Those conversations about the railway contracts, and which of the two towns would still exist at the turn of the century. It seemed that everyone thought of it as an either-or thing: if the Landing did well, then the Fort would fail and disappear, and if the Fort did well, as it had in the old days, before the Hudson's Bay Company gave up on it, well then the Landing would disappear into the Bay. Or something like that.

Mr. Campbell leaned back now, so that his chair stood on its hind legs. He thrust one hand in his trousers pocket. "People think the Landing is a bad place; people have too much fun. But let me tell you – and I know from experience – that crawling into the earth is not a pleasurable thing. Sometimes, when you crawl out at the end of the day, you have to go to some bright, loud place, just to remind yourself that you're alive. Maybe the Fort Willy people don't understand that. Maybe they don't understand a bit of merriment." He brought the chair down with a crack of wood on wood. "But let me tell you! They do understand how to get what they want – like a spoiled child – especially from the government. What about that deal the Town Plotters made? Selling eight dollar land for five hundred dollars an acre? And they accuse the Landing people of debauchery and gambling! Ha!"

Oliver wasn't sure what debauchery meant, but he knew it couldn't be good. Miss Darbyshire had been tugging on that cuff all the time that Mr. Campbell was speaking. Now, angrily, he pulled away from her.

"Am I wrong?" he asked her.

"No – those are the facts," she answered.

"Well!" Mr. Campbell looked smug.

"It's just that those aren't the only facts." Now she looked at Oliver.

"No?" Mr. Campbell wasn't going to let this go.

"No!" she said.

"And what are the other facts, ma'am?" asked Mr. Campbell.

"Those are the facts of certain business people. There are also the facts of the rest of the people. And the rest of the people don't care." She pointed at Mr. Campbell. "Only you care. You take part in the schemimg. You fuel the competition and hatred, like adding wood to a fire. Then you sit there and blow on the fire, till it burns you up, and turns you into a mean and angry person, and leaves you friendless." Miss Darbyshire looked as if she was about to cry. Mr. Campbell just looked very red – the way he looked when he was angry.

"I don't take part in the scheming, as you put it!"

"Maybe not in the way that those business-men do – the men you claim to despise," she said. "But you take part in your own way."

Mr. Campbell didn't have an answer for her this time. In fact, Oliver thought he looked rather tired.

"I believe that someday these two towns are going to be one great city!" Miss Darbyshire sat very straight and tall.

"Bah! It'll never happen. People here'd never be able to decide on a name ... what would they call it? Fort Prince Arthur William? Ha!" Mr. Campbell shook his head.

"Maybe they'll call it something else alto-gether. Maybe..." she thought a moment. "Maybe Thunder Bay. We do *all* live on the Bay. You have no hope, Clifford Campbell." She stood up from the table, and didn't wait for Mr. Campbell to pull out her chair. "Let's go." She placed her hand under Mr. Campbell's arm and pulled him to his feet.

They left before Bert and his parents did, and Oliver passed his cousin's table without looking at him, even though doing so meant that he wasn't watching where he was going, and he bumped into the sideboard that stood in the middle of the front wall.

"Goodbye, Oliver," sang out the thin voice of his Aunt Emily. Oliver wished her voice didn't sound as sad as it did.

Oliver and Mr. Campbell bid Miss Darbyshire goodnight outside her home and then returned to the rooms next to the blacksmith shop.

Mr. Campbell lighted an oil lamp, poured himself another bit of whiskey, and warmed milk on the stove for Oliver. Then he reached for a small wooden box on a shelf over the window and sat at the table across from Oliver.

He opened the box. "I'll teach you to play with the cards – but you must only play." He raised one brow. "Your father would not be a happy man if I taught you to gamble."

Another time, saying this, he would have sounded mocking, but not that night. He silently shuffled and dealt the cards, and did so with such skill that Oliver felt clumsy simply holding them.

But Mr. Campbell seemed to perk up as he lighted a pipe, leaned back from the table, and placed a card down. He even began to whistle around the pipe stem and through the gaps between his teeth. "Aye," he said, "we will do our work tomorrow, won't we, Oliver?"

Oliver nodded, and fumbled with the cards in his hand. Mr. Campbell stared at him suddenly, which made Oliver even more self-conscious of his clumsiness, but when he spoke, Mr. Campbell said nothing about Oliver and his cards.

"Miss Darbyshire's a kind woman, is she not?" he said, and he didn't seem to want an answer, so Oliver didn't give him one. And those were the last words he said that night. He didn't explain the game they played, but expected Oliver to follow from his example, and when he'd decided they were done, he climbed the loft to his bed.

Oliver curled up in the quilt that the black-smith had left for him on the bench.

This time in his dream he knew right away that he was at the dock in Liverpool. The grey shadow of the ship angled over him once more.

This time, there were only the voices and shouts of the dock hands and others; no one called his name.

Oliver stood still in the midst of the bustle and under the wall of the ship and, though he was surrounded by people, he felt completely alone.

Bert's boot, he remembered, and he set off in that direction. "I'm coming!" he yelled. No one yelled in return. He rounded the corner where he'd last seen the boot – Bert's foot – at the bottom of a jumble of shipping crates, but the boot was gone. Bert was gone. Everything was gone.

The grey ship pulled past him, bound for a new place.

Oliver awoke to hear Mr. Campbell's breathing, rattling like an old boat above him in the loft.

The following day, Mr. Campbell began to teach Oliver the trade of blacksmithing. "Maybe you'll apprentice with me," he said at one point.

Maybe, thought Oliver. He was growing used to the man's silence as they worked, his outbursts as he drank his coffee or something else, and his brusque commands. It had never occurred to Oliver to become a blacksmith; he'd always taken for granted that he'd be a book-binder like his father and grandfather. Now he thought, maybe.

"'Course I can't pay a good wage, but I can pay. And I think that in a couple of years, when the business has built up, there'll be enough work to keep a boy busy."

At the end of the workday – midafternoon so that he could return home in daylight – Mr.

Campbell asked for the envelope he'd given Oliver the week before. And this time he put fifteen cents in, and handed it back.

"Take care of that family of yours," he said, and with those few words, he let Oliver know that he knew all about Father being on the nitroglycerin trail.

As he headed home, Oliver took the coins out of the envelope, which he folded carefully and put in the pocket of his shirt, safe for next week. He wrapped his fingers around the coins in his jacket pocket. He could feel their weight and hear their music. He thought of Old Mac. With the coins in hand, the horse seemed closer to him somehow. Next week, if Mr. Campbell continued to pay him fifteen cents, Oliver would have forty. He wondered how much Mr. Phillips had paid his father.

He'd almost reached the end of Cumberland Street, when he decided to turn around. A thought had occurred to him. What if Mr. Phillips was planning to resell Old Mac? What if he'd done so already? Old Mac might be gone now. Oliver hadn't thought of that before. Perhaps he ought to speak to Mr. Phillips and ask him if he could wait for Oliver to be able to pay him back.

Oliver knew that Mr. Phillips lived in the same boarding house that Miss Darbyshire lived in.

Widow Lucas, who ran the boarding house, answered his knock.

"Mr. Phillips?" she said, "he's out back, in the stable."

So Oliver went around the side of the two-storey, white clapboard building to the back, where there was a large shed that Mr. Phillips was using as a stable. He was feeding three horses. Old Mac was not one of them.

"It's you," Mr. Phillips said, as he straightened up and saw Oliver.

"I came to see Mac," said Oliver. Inside his pocket, his fingers still curled around the coins, hoping, hoping.

"He's gone." Mr. Phillips began to chip the ice in the horses' drinking trough.

"Gone where?"

Mr. Phillips squinted at Oliver. "He should be plodding east by now."

Again, east! "When did he leave? Who bought him?"

"Last Sunday." Mr. Phillips laughed then. "And no one bought that old nag! I hired him out."

Oliver's fingers tightened, and he turned quickly, and was gone as soon as he heard the last of Mr. Phillips's words.

At the edge of town, he stopped to fasten his snowshoes. His head was pounding. Slowly he looked up. He held his breath to try to make the pounding stop. But when he exhaled and took another breath, which he had to do, the pounding grew worse. He stood up, and began to plod home.

The pieces were beginning to come together. Old Mac and Father, Mr. Phillips and the nitroglycerin trail.

Mr. Phillips must have been buying old, worn-out horses, then turning around and hiring them out to the men who organized the trail. The horses were probably used to carry the supplies that the men could not.

The other horses that Oliver knew of – Nellie and Trotmore – were also old like Mac. If they were able to make more than one or two trips, Mr. Phillips would probably consider himself lucky. And if they died on the trail, or were blown sky high by the explosives, no one would miss them. Old horses were like men with hungry families: there were always more.

The pounding in Oliver's head began to subside, especially as he discovered one comforting thought; his father and Old Mac were together on the trail. They would keep each other company.

Oliver could see his home now, just a chimney appearing over the rise of a gentle hill, above the scruffy pines and sad aspen, a narrow trail of smoke angling away in the wind. A lump was in his throat as it had been at the last sight of the kitchen back home.

Oliver remembered the day that his family had left Liverpool. He remembered turning back to see the kitchen – his favourite room – and what he'd seen was a bare, dark place. He hadn't realized that it was that dark. The fire in the stove was out, the smells of tea and soup were almost passed, and the city smell of burning coal was taking over, creeping under the door and through every chink in the place. Without the people, the room was no longer home. That's when Oliver had known he was going to have to make Canada home. The people who mattered to him most would be there.

But now Father and Bert and Old Mac weren't, and he knew he would see little of Uncle Will and Aunt Emily, except when he bumped into them. Oliver didn't know how or if he could fix things. Maybe the pieces were already missing and he'd never be able to put them back together. That's how it was beginning to feel.

The sight of that thin chimney with its struggling smoke tail made him feel terribly alone, and he cried.

Chapter 9

THE WEEK FELT EVEN LONGER THAN THE ONE before. Father had been quite certain that he'd be home by Friday or, at the latest, Saturday. Oliver told himself that it wasn't that long until then, but as Monday crawled reluctantly to Tuesday, and Tuesday circled madly trying to avoid Wednesday, Oliver began to think that the end of the week would never come.

Wednesday at school, Miss Groom seemed to talk slowly, explaining sums and reading aloud. Oliver didn't hear the story, even though he usually tried to remember it so that he could share it with Hannah later. But that day all he could think of was Father, out there in the snow somewhere, and he hoped and hoped that he was coming home. He tried to concentrate on what Miss Groom was saying. He gave up and was glad when the teacher sent them home.

There he found Mum out of breath, dancing around the main room of the house. For a moment he thought he'd missed the last two weeks – Mum was so happy.

"I did something today, Oliver!" she said.

Oliver guessed that she hadn't broken anything.

"I sent a telegram from the CPR office to Aunt Emily!" She clapped her hands like a child. "I don't know why I didn't think to do that before now. I'm always too busy to walk to the Landing, and I've missed her so much … I'm going to go to Mr. Kruger's and ask him if I can borrow Belle and the cutter tomorrow morning."

Oliver had taken his coat off as soon as he entered the house. Now he put it back on.

"I'll do that for you, Mum." The last sound he heard as he closed the heavy door behind him was the sound of Mum's laughter. She was so pleased at the thought of seeing Aunt Emily. They hadn't seen each other at all since the fight, and since Father had sold Old Mac.

Oliver hadn't told Mum about the way he'd disappeared with the Krugers' horse and cutter, and even though it seemed that Mr. Kruger was understanding, Oliver still felt a bit awkward.

As he reached the farmer's front gate, Mr. Kruger came from around the back of the house, a bucket of scraps in his hand. He smiled when he saw Oliver and motioned for him to follow.

"I'm off to the barn. Come see Belle and Pepper."

Oliver followed him into the warmth of the small barn. Mr. Kruger handed him the pail. "This is for the pig," he said. Oliver went to the far corner and filled the pig's trough with the scraps. Mr. Kruger worked, replacing hay for Belle.

"When do you expect your father home?" he asked, and at the mention of his father, the fear in Oliver started up again.

"Some time this Friday or Saturday, sir," said Oliver.

"Not a long trip then, is it?"

"Long enough." Each day felt as long as the voyage across the Atlantic all over again, but Oliver didn't say that to Mr. Kruger.

Mr. Kruger looked hard at him as he reached for the pail that Oliver held. "I don't suppose you came here to feed my pig," he said.

"No." Oliver took a deep breath. "I came to see if my Mum might borrow your cutter tomorrow. She'd like to go to the Landing to see my aunt. And I think it might ease her mind."

"I see – what time would this be?"

Oliver thought a moment. "Whenever it's available."

"Is Old Mac ill, Oliver?"

"No, sir. Father sold him."

"But you need something to drive." Mr. Kruger pursed his lips as he thought. "Tell your

Mum that I will fetch her at lunch hour. I will take her to the Landing, and first thing Friday morning, you can use Belle and the cutter to fetch her back. But it must be first thing – I need Belle to haul some ice from the lake."

Oliver nodded. "First thing, Mr. Kruger. And thank you."

Oliver wondered what would happen when Mum and Aunt Emily finally spent time together. Would it all come out ... the fighting, Uncle Will's job offer, even Oliver's sharing dinner with Mr. Campbell and Miss Darbyshire? He tried not to think about it. He couldn't keep Mum and Aunt Emily apart forever, although just a bit longer would be nice.

He had to admit that a little part of him had hoped that Mr. Kruger wouldn't be able to loan Mum the cutter. But that was not to be. Mr. Kruger was a nice man; he'd even forgiven Oliver for "borrowing" his sleigh.

After dinner, the family pulled close to the stove and Eliza dragged over a small table and set up the dominoes. Oliver for once didn't play, but stood back, leaning against the rough wall of the cabin. This was the exact spot where his father always leaned, and Oliver's body didn't fit into the space between the floor and the railing which ran around the room. The railing reached his father's waist and he could comfortably rest his elbow on it, but for Oliver the railing butted into his neck. He gave up and climbed the ladder to the loft.

The light was dim but he knew where to feel for his money jar. It rattled gently as he picked it up. He put his hand into his pocket, pulled out the fifteen cents, added it to the ten, and replaced the jar behind the foot of his bed. He sat on the floor with his back against the bed, listening to the click of dominoes and watching the lamplight flicker through the spaces between the floorboards, as he did at night before his parents went to bed. Usually the sight of that glow from the floor cheered him or at least made him feel comfortable. Tonight, his thoughts stood in the way of any comfort he might feel.

"Oliver?" Mum called him. "What are you doing? Come down and play with us."

"Soon," he answered. He didn't tell her what he was doing.

He reached back for the jar, emptied the coins into his hand, and felt them as if they might have an answer.

What if he'd told Father about working for Mr. Campbell? Might he have not gone?

Realistically, Oliver knew that ten or fifteen cents was not enough for his family to live on. His father would have gone even if he'd known that Oliver had a job. But still Oliver felt guilty. Maybe the bit of money he'd earned would have been enough until his father found a job here in town.

Oliver could hear Mum below, singing. She'd worked so hard at keeping her spirits up for the past ten days so as not to frighten the other children, but Oliver had seen through her efforts. Probably because he'd been doing the same himself.

But what about Old Mac? It was quite possible that Oliver would never see Mac again. That was a long trip for an old horse. But if he gave the money to Mum, wasn't that like giving up on his friend? He felt that by not saving the money for Old Mac, he was in some way saying goodbye to him.

Oliver wrapped his fingers around the coins one last time. He knew what he had to do, but that didn't make it any easier. "I'll get you back somehow, Mac," he promised. Then he climbed down the ladder, the coins in one fist.

Eliza and Alberta had just finished their game, which Gavin had watched and Hannah had cheered. Now Eliza was stacking the black and white pieces of wood.

"Perhaps you can put on your nightshirts," suggested Mum from her corner seat. She held a mug of tea in her hands as if to warm them. Usually she insisted on tea in a cup.

No one, not even Gavin, had argued with Mum lately, and now the three younger children climbed the ladder without protest and Hannah crawled into her mother's bed in the adjoining room. Oliver sat down next to the domino table. He picked up one of the smooth rectangles – he'd always liked the feel of the dominoes – and stood it on its end.

"Mum," he began, "I need to tell you something." He stood a second domino next to the first, and then a third. The coins were still in his fist.

"I have a bit of money," he said and laid the coins out next to the dominoes. Mum didn't say anything.

"I've been working for Mr. Campbell." He set up a fourth and fifth domino and wondered how far he would have to go with his explanation. He didn't want to lie. It seemed that one thing always led to another: Father's fight, Oliver and Bert's fight, lying about seeing Aunt Emily, guilt about the coins....

Oliver poked the first domino with the tip of his finger and, one after the other, all five rattled onto the tabletop.

"I was hoping to buy back Old Mac," he said.

Mum nodded slowly. "I'd like to have Mac back," she said.

"But we're going to need food, and oil for the lamps and...." Oliver said, his voice drifting off as Mum continued nodding.

"I still have some money from the five dollars they paid your father – perhaps we can save your coins as emergency money." Mum stood up to reach for the tea which was in a cooking pot on the table.

Oliver waited for her questions, but they didn't come. Perhaps she was so used to his father's reluctance to speak of anything important that she didn't think to ask.

The children, in their nightshirts, climbed down the ladder to say goodnight to Mum. Eliza looked strangely at Oliver and he knew that she'd heard every word of the conversation.

"You'd best go to bed too," said Mum to Oliver, when the others were gone. Oliver kissed her goodnight, and began to climb the ladder after his brother and sisters. He stopped halfway up.

"Mr. Campbell's not so grumpy, you know. He says maybe I can apprentice with him someday."

"He says that, does he?" said Mum, her eyebrows raised. Then she smiled slightly.

Under his quilt, Oliver turned to find a comfortable position.

Eliza's voice came out of the darkness. "Mr. Campbell's not so grumpy, eh? I don't believe it."

But Oliver heard the rhythmic breathing of her sleep before he could think of a word to say.

The light between the floorboards flickered for a long time that night, much longer than usual.

Mum was bundled in her warmest wool things and all the children stood shivering in the doorway to see her off. It wasn't often that their mother left them for any period of time. Hannah clung to Oliver's trouser leg, but Gavin slipped back into the house even before the cutter pulled away and ladled his own bowl of soup from the pot on the stove. After Eliza closed the door behind everyone, they all sat down and ate a late lunch, and the remainder of the day was long and drifted like a rope swing in the wind.

Oliver awoke the next morning with a new sensation in his belly. The familiar fear was there, but now it had uncurled and sat bolt upright. It seemed ready, sniffing and listening for something.

But that was just a thought really – nothing Oliver could put into words. What he could put into words was the thought of his father.

Today was the day he was to return. Oliver couldn't wait another day. It had to be today.

It was still dark outside. It might have been the middle of the night, but Oliver was quite certain that he could not go back to sleep. He was very quiet as he felt for his footing down the ladder, and it was odd not to feel Hannah's little hands reaching for him. No doubt she was still sound asleep between Eliza and Alberta; she'd slept in the loft last night instead of in her usual place – the trundle bed in their parents' room downstairs.

He lighted an oil lamp – just a tiny flame – and waited for the glass globe to warm before he made the flame grow. And he made coffee for himself for the first time and, not knowing how to measure the beans, he made it terribly strong. He took a first sip, and blinked, and muttered to himself, as there was no one else who might hear.

Oliver shook his head. "I'm beginning to sound like Mr. Campbell," he said aloud. "Next thing, I'll be moaning and muttering about 'these damned towns.'" He took another sip, and wondered if he might ever really be like Mr. Campbell. How did a person become like that? grumpy and angry about almost everything? How did a person become friendless?

Even as he asked himself this question, Oliver began to see an answer. That is, he began to see that he could become Mr. Campbell. After all, he'd ruined the one most important friendship he had. And he'd cursed this place for forcing his father from his family. In less than three weeks, Oliver had been more angry than he'd ever been. Maybe he'd become the Grump of Fort William.

Another swallow of coffee and he poured it back into the pot. He pulled on an extra pair of knitted socks and his boots, sweater, and jacket. This time of day was the coldest.

It must be close to the time when he should pick up the cutter at Krugers, he thought. He extinguished the flame in the lamp and pulled on the new mitts that Mum had made for him. They were warm and dyed a brilliant red, but Oliver still missed his old favourite mitts which he'd lost the day that he and Bert had argued. He wondered if perhaps Bert had found them, and wished he had the courage to go and ask. The lost mitts would be a perfect excuse to go and speak with Bert, and maybe they could straighten this out. "You're daydreaming," he muttered again. The situation was too far gone for something as simple as lost mittens to fix it.

He let himself out the door, where he fastened his snowshoes and began the walk to the farm.

"Carry me, Olver." He heard a tiny voice, and there was Hannah, bundled in almost every outdoor piece of clothing that Eliza and Alberta owned. "Take me with you," she said.

"I didn't hear you getting dressed," was all he could think of to say.

"You were talking to yourself," Hannah said, and Oliver felt quite foolish.

"*I'm* your friend, Olver. Take me with you."

"I can't take you, Hannah. I won't be able to hurry if you're with me, and Mr. Kruger needs Belle back as soon as possible."

His sister looked as if she was about to cry. Oliver picked her up and held her close. "Don't cry, Hannah. Your tears will freeze. I'll build up the fire in the stove before I go, so that the house is warm. The others will wake up and you can all wait together for me to bring Mum home." He hoped his words would comfort her. He carried her back into the house and added two logs to the stove which had been left burning low all night. The fire roared with morning warmth. Oliver secured the stove door and left the draft open slightly.

He pulled one chair close, another for Hannah to rest her feet on, and set her on the wooden seat with a blanket tucked around her.

"There. You wait for me. I won't be long." He kissed the top of her head, and left.

But no sooner was he out the door and starting to the farm when he again heard that voice. "Olver! I'm coming with you!" And there she was, running along at his side, her mittened hands waving in the air.

The hour was passing quickly. Oliver didn't have time to take Hannah back to the house. He'd have to wake up Eliza so that she could make certain Hannah didn't follow him again.

No, he didn't have the time. So he crouched low and she climbed on his back. Then he stood with her looking over his head, clinging to his neck, and they continued to the Krugers.

Mr. Kruger had Belle and the cutter waiting for them.

"I see you brought someone to keep you company," he said as he watched Oliver help his sister into the cutter and climb in himself. Mr. Kruger leaned over and helped pull the bearskin around the two of them, then he handed the reins to Oliver.

Belle started off at a good clip, pulling towards the Landing. Today she wasn't side-tracked as she'd been that Sunday, and she seemed happy to be moving so early on this cold January morning.

Today Father might return. Anything could happen today. Anything at all.

Oliver wished there was a particular time at which his father was supposed to return, but it could be any time. Late in the night, or early. He could be arriving this very moment. Oliver wondered if he would have to go first to the Powder Company office or if he would be able to come directly home.

"When will Father be home?" asked Hannah.

Oliver wondered if he was still talking out loud to himself.

"Soon," he said, with more hope than he felt.

They were nearing the Landing now. A few windows of early risers showed orange light and there was a soft glow in the east. Oliver could see the outlines of log and clapboard homes. With the sun rising, the white shapes were like ghosts. The hotels, the boarding houses, the church bell tower, all loomed in the strange light and seemed oversized and odd-shaped, with angles that appeared to be twisted. It was eerie, but even so, Oliver couldn't help thinking of how much he enjoyed being awake at this magical hour. They passed the Powder Company. All seemed quiet, though he kept looking back, half hoping.

There were a few clouds in the sky and their outlines reflected the glow of the rising sun. A gentle wind pushed the clouds, but not hurriedly. Oliver looked back again, peering into the dim light of early morning. Surely it wasn't ... that looked like smoke – not cloud – drifting from one of the offices of the Powder Company.

Oliver stood in the moving cutter. It was smoke! There was a fire at the Powder Company. If it were to spread to the magazine where the explosives were stored....

Oliver pulled hard on Belle's reins, up Arthur Street, past his cousin's home. He must get to the church and ring the bell. *Ring the bell. Sound the alarm.*

Prince Arthur's Landing was a night town.

In the morning the town slept and the streets were empty, even Arthur Street. Oliver reached to his left, to the side of the cutter where he'd noticed Mr. Kruger kept a whip. He pulled it out now and when Belle felt the ends of it on her back she almost flew down the stretch of road towards the church and the bell tower. Hannah, still wrapped in the bearskin, clung to Oliver as the horse dragged the cutter at a wild pace.

Then Belle caught the scent of fire. She turned so abruptly that the cutter overturned. She reared, throwing her front hooves in the air, snorting, her eyes wild and circling.

Oliver and Hannah tumbled to the ground and Belle pulled the cutter away in the direction of her home. They lay there, stunned for a moment. Then Oliver picked himself up. He bent over Hannah, put both hands on her shoulders under the bearskin, and said: "Don't move – I'll be right back."

He ran towards the church, faster and faster, up the front steps, grabbing for the wooden handrail to keep from slipping. He flung open the front door, slid across the polished wood floor to the door that led to the bell tower. Opened that and climbed up, up, up. There was the rope of the bell. He grabbed it with both hands. He could barely move it. Just a bit, and the momentum carried it. He pulled again, waited for it to swing, and again. It was ringing,

ringing loud, again and again, a warning, then echoing. That would have to be enough. Back down the narrow, twisted stairs. He left the front door open behind him. Back to Hannah waiting in the snow.

But the bearskin was empty. Hannah was gone.

Chapter 10

WINDOWS OPENED AND DOORS, AND A MURMUR of voices could be heard growing louder, and then a shout. "The Powder Company – there's a fire!"

"Fire!" another yell.

All along Arthur Street the sounds of voices grew. "Who rang the bell?" Oliver heard someone shout.

He didn't answer. He was staring at the ground at his feet where Hannah had been just seconds before. She can't be far, he told himself, looking around and hoping to see Alberta's red knitted hat. "Hannah!" he called for her once. And again, "Hannah!" He looked for her footprints, but in the roadway the snow was packed and hard and he could see nothing.

People began to come out of their homes and from the boarding houses and the hotels: miners in their long johns, businessmen in their suspenders, women, one with a baby crying. They didn't seem to notice Oliver there as they swept by, heading down Cumberland Street, Court Street, Water Street, in the direction of the factory.

Oliver noticed the face of a girl staring out through a window of one of the hotels. She wasn't rushing down the stairs, through the door, like the others. She caught Oliver looking at her, and she waved and smiled. Oliver started to raise his hand.

"It could blow!" someone called out.

"Aye – it could blow!" Oliver turned as he heard Mr. Campbell's voice in the melee.

"Mr. Campbell!" Oliver shouted, but with little hope of being heard as people pushed between him and the blacksmith.

Then the earth trembled.

Just a little tremble, as if it felt only a cold finger at the back of its neck. A tremble of surprise and fear. A shake really. Oliver wasn't certain he'd felt anything at all.

There it was again, more powerful this time. And a rumble that was not thunder. The rumble did not stop but grew loud and angry and the earth shook, as if the finger that had touched the back of its neck was now some creature clinging to its back that must be shaken off. The air filled with sounds: shouts, screams, and sounds he couldn't recognize – sounds that were almost musical. Shattering glass. Every so often as the earth lurched the church bell tolled – an echo of his earlier warning.

"Mr. Campbell!" Oliver shouted again, and thought that the blacksmith's head half turned in his direction. "Have you seen my sister? Hannah – she's missing!" But Mr. Campbell appeared not to hear. He moved alongside the crowd, waving his arms like a choirmaster, urging them to move in the same direction, and away from the Powder Company. "All together now!" he bellowed. "Everyone together!" But no one paid any attention to him, and they continued to run back and forth. Some seemed to be going in circles. There were shouts, and hands thrust into the air as fingers pointed to the grey smoke, mushrooming from the little office building

Oliver pushed his way towards the blacksmith, but Mr. Campbell had turned away from the people, and Oliver recognized the deep shrug of his shoulders and saw his hands raised in the air. Mr. Campbell shook his hands as if to rid himself of "the crazy people," as he always called them. Oliver could imagine what he must be mumbling under his breath.

The crowd swirled between them and Oliver lost sight of Mr. Campbell. When he was able to see him again, Mr. Campbell had turned and was staring at the girl still standing in the hotel window. Again Oliver tried to reach him, but he stumbled and tripped over a boot in his path. When he was upright again, Mr. Campbell was gone and there – farther down the street – was a flash of red hat moving towards the dry goods store. Perhaps Hannah would have the sense to head for the store and her mother. But even as he thought this and moved quickly, Oliver knew that she probably wouldn't recognize the store, nor any of the streets. The odd time that she'd come to the Landing she was usually asleep in Mum's arms in a borrowed buggy.

The sky darkened with grey smoke clouds. It was as if the clock had suddenly gone backward and was retreating into the night.

Oliver set off after Hannah, following the flame of hat as she weaved down the street, moving along the boardwalks, sometimes disappearing down side streets only to reappear on Arthur Street, and always managing to stay ahead of Oliver. Sometimes he tried to run to catch up to her, but the people still came from their doors and pressed against him, always moving in the opposite direction. Somehow little Hannah managed to slip between. Oliver watched over someone's shoulder as she passed by Uncle Will's store without so much as a glance at it.

And then she disappeared completely. Oliver reached for the person who blocked his path and pushed past, and for an instant he had a clear view of the roadway before it again filled with people. He could not see his sister. He went down side streets – north and south – and back to Arthur Street. He continued all the way to the waterfront, away from the crowd, and down the length of dock. Then he turned and looked south.

The town looked as if it might be crushed by the weight of the clouds pressing down upon it, billowing like sails and rolling like the sea. He walked slowly up the dock, his mind churning.

Then there was a boom like nothing that Oliver had ever heard. For a split second he thought that perhaps the Sleeping Giant, the Thunder God, had awakened and was rising with a roar to his stony feet. Oliver wrapped his arms around his head and fell to the ground. Keeping his head down so that all he saw before him was the dirty white of the packed snow, he crawled on his belly along the street.

"Hannah!" he called, barely aware of what he was doing. He didn't know he was sobbing.

The booming continued and, with great effort, Oliver pulled himself to his knees in the middle of the roadway. He felt he was being watched – the Thunder God had opened his eyes – but when he slowly looked around him, he realized that the street was lined with the gaping eyes of blown-out windows, and every door stood dark and open, staring after the people who had left them behind or amazed at the force that had broken them so rudely.

The clouds were beginning to lift, carried by the wind, and Oliver struggled to his feet to see past the buildings of Cumberland Street, past the grey sails and sea clouds, to the Powder Company buildings.

They were gone.

He thought perhaps he'd looked in the wrong direction. He turned. The Giant was still in his place, sleeping. Oliver turned back again.

No. They were gone – the main building, the office, the magazine where the explosives were stored – everything was gone.

What if his father had come home early? What if he was at the Powder Company? What if...?

He thought perhaps he should also be moving in the direction that the others did, but the questions he had about his father frightened him and he wasn't ready for the answers yet. Besides, Hannah was still missing.

Hannah. He had to find Hannah.

"And I need help," he said aloud as he headed back in the direction of the dry goods store.

Chapter 11

BERT. HE NEEDED BERT. BERT ALWAYS FOUND what he was looking for.

Oliver's stubbornness cracked like dried mud on the sole of a boot, and crumbled away under his feet as he ran to find his cousin.

He didn't look at the people as they passed. They were a grey mass, like the ship in his dream. Was this another dream? Would it be like the last, with no trace of Bert?

"Bert!" he called out as he made his way to the dry goods store. There was the front door; he could see it now, an empty black doorway. Somehow the sign that Uncle Will had hung over a nail had stayed, and it read CLOSED, though the glass was gone.

It was going to be like his dream. No one would be there. There wouldn't be so much as a boot.

Then there was Bert, staring at Oliver from around the corner of the store.

"Bert!" Oliver ran after his cousin. "Bert – I need your help – Hannah's missing." Oliver's eyes were watering, and not from the smoke. Nothing mattered now except finding Hannah. The past two weeks didn't change that fact. He needed Bert. "Bert, we have to find her...." Oliver felt lightheaded. He was so scared.

Bert grasped Oliver's arm, just above his wrist. "Have you checked the dock? And the fishing holes? The ice holes?" Even as he spoke, Bert moved towards the Bay.

"I just came from there."

Bert stopped abruptly and Oliver lurched to a stop next to him.

"Hannah's afraid of crowds, isn't she?" Bert asked.

Oliver nodded. Bert was so logical.

"So she would have gone away from the crowd," he continued.

"That would be in the direction of the docks," Oliver pointed out.

"Yes – but she didn't get that far." Bert stood very still. If Oliver hadn't known better, he would have thought that Bert was wasting time, but he watched his cousin. He knew how Bert's mind worked.

"She disappeared close to here," said Oliver.

Bert turned around slowly. "Maybe she saw the people coming from their doors, and maybe she hid in the first place she saw."

Hannah hiding. That was not a possibility that Oliver wanted to think about. Not in this cold weather. What if she fell asleep? Aunt Emily was always warning the children about that drowsy warmth they would feel before they began to freeze. People would fall asleep with the false warmth and.... Oliver shook his head and breathed deeply. Bert was still turning slowly and thinking.

Oliver imitated his cousin and turned as well, trying to imagine how this place would appear to his little sister. He kneeled. What would look safe to Hannah?

And then he knew. Oliver went to the circle of cedar trees and pulled back the branches, heavy with snow, and saw a flash of red through the green and white. A thought went quickly through his mind: red would always be his favourite colour.

Hannah was sound asleep, her hair across her tear-streaked face. She moaned when Oliver picked her up, as if she'd been crying as she fell asleep and a sob was left unfinished in her throat.

Oliver carried her through the blown-out doorway of the dry goods store, being careful not to touch the sharp edges of broken glass, and went up the stairs. Bert followed closely.

Mum and Aunt Emily stood at the top of the stairs, but Mum rushed down as Oliver began to climb with Hannah, and reached for her. As

Mum lifted his sister's weight from his arms, Oliver felt suddenly weak and like a rag doll.

"What has happened? Is she all right?"

Oliver managed to nod. "She's asleep – she's wearing every piece of outdoor clothing that Eliza and Alberta own. I think she's quite warm."

"She's asleep? Is that all? I thought there was some accident…."

"No. No accident. She went missing when I … left her … to ring the bell."

When Oliver said the word "missing," his mother tightened her hold of Hannah. But she didn't say anything about that. Instead she said: "You rang the bell?"

"Yes." Still feeling weak, Oliver held his hand to the wall for support and followed his mother and Aunt Emily into the kitchen.

Bert cleared a large sewing basket from the bench near the fire and Mum laid Hannah down and pulled her boots off.

"It was very brave of you to ring the bell, Oliver."

Oliver didn't respond. Now that he was there, standing in the middle of his aunt's kitchen, he realized how much he'd missed that place. The golden warmth of the fire, the smell of drying wool, mittens and socks hanging on their rack to the side of the blaze, the biscuit jar always full. And there were his father's books, neatly side by side in a small wooden crate. Uncle Will hadn't sold them.

Mum was massaging Hannah's feet and the little girl lay there, silent and watchful.

"Where's Pa?" Bert asked his mother.

Aunt Emily was busy preparing tea. "Your father went out as soon as he heard the bell ring." She stopped for a moment. Oliver's mother noticed her stillness and looked up at her.

"What is it, Emily?"

"It's so quiet," Aunt Emily whispered. Oliver suddenly realized how quiet it was. The booming had stopped, the dreadful thuds that sounded like they could only be the footfalls of the Thunder God – all had stopped. Oliver hadn't even noticed when. Hannah sat up slowly. "What's everyone listening to? I don't hear anything!"

Mum laughed softly and reached for her hand. "Exactly. We're listening to the silence, Hannah."

Hannah looked puzzled. "Oh," she said.

Aunt Emily resumed her tea making. "You found Hannah in good time. She's very tired, but she seems warm enough. And she can wiggle her toes!" Emily laughed gently. "Did she wake up early this morning? She might have slept there for hours and not noticed the cold."

She took a pair of knitted slippers from the rack by the fire and handed them to Mum, who pulled them over Hannah's feet.

Then Aunt Emily passed a wide-mouthed mug of mostly milk to Hannah, who wrapped both hands around it and lifted it to her lips. Her entire face disappeared as she drank.

Mum accepted the dainty teacup that Emily handed to her and stood up, moving towards the window that overlooked the street. "Will should be back soon," she said, and there was a wistful tone to her words. "I hope no one's been hurt."

"I hope not," Aunt Emily echoed Mum's words as she filled two more large mugs for Bert and Oliver, and gently pried Hannah's from her hands – she was falling asleep again, cosy now from the fire. Emily followed Mum and stood behind her, peering out the narrow window.

Oliver and Bert were left facing each other.

Oliver wanted to thank Bert for his help in finding Hannah, but he didn't speak. Neither did Bert.

The silence filled every corner of the room.

Finally, Bert gave Oliver a half-twisted smile and then turned his attention to a shirt that was lying crumpled in the basket next to the bench. He picked up a jar of buttons, opened it, and kneeling, spread them out on the small table. He laid the shirt out. There were three buttons missing. "Do you think any one of these matches?" Bert put several buttons on the brown cloth.

"That one is quite close." Oliver pointed out one mottled cream-coloured button. He felt foolish doing this. Why couldn't they talk about the fight? He almost wished that Bert would pick up some crockery and throw it, instead of doing this: a mundane chore. He thought of all the times he'd seen Mum do exactly that – buttons or darning or knitting – when something was bothering her, and he understood why she'd broken her precious teapot.

So he kneeled next to Bert and helped him look through the collection in the jar. They spread the tiny discs of shell and wood, and once in awhile their hands or shoulders brushed as they leaned over the table.

The street outside was filled with clamour again – voices talking, shouting, returning from the direction of the explosion. Oliver looked up to see Mum standing in the doorway from the front room.

"He's here," was all she said, looking towards the entrance door.

Then the door burst open and it was Uncle Will, so tall he filled the door frame and ducked his head slightly as he entered. His face was smudged and the front of his coat was dark with soot, but his teeth were wide and white and his brown eyes glistened. Then he stepped away from the doorway and into the room. There, on the top step, his face also smudged except for

126

two streaks where tears had passed and his ruddy skin shone through ... there was....

"Father!" The fear in Oliver's belly uncurled so quickly that the force of it made him leap towards his father. He circled his arms around his father's chest, and felt the worn leather of his father's coat at his cheek.

The men on the nitroglycerin trail had seen the explosion from two miles away. "Had we been just a half-hour earlier...." Oliver's father shook his head as he spoke.

"It's a miracle," said Aunt Emily.

Father took a long sip of coffee and pulled his pressed-back chair even closer to the stove, as if he felt a chill he could not get rid of. "It had more to do with Old Mac than a miracle, Emily."

"What do you mean?" asked Oliver. "Where is Old Mac?"

"First question answered first." Another sip. "We were on the trail early this morning – when it was still dark almost. 'We' being those of us who made it. We were forty-two strong when we left, and thirty-three coming back." He paused.

"Anyway. Old Mac wasn't doing too well after a week of carrying more than he's ever carried before, but he was going along. And then he stopped. I didn't notice and no one else did either. I don't know why he stopped. We kept moving and then Brian McPhee noticed – he's something like our Gavin – always hungry. In fact, if Old Mac hadn't been carrying all of the food that was left, no one would have noticed till we returned home. Anyway, McPhee let out a shout and of course, when I realized it was Mac that was missing, both of us insisted we go back. And we did. Which made us late by almost exactly half an hour."

Mum exhaled loudly.

"And where is Mac?" asked Oliver.

His father examined the draft on the stove. "I guess he couldn't take the load any more, son. When we went back we found that he'd slid down the side of the trail. I went down to where he was, at the bottom near the river, but there was nothing I could do for him."

"Was he in pain?" asked Oliver. There might have been only him and his father in the room right then.

"No. He wasn't in pain any more."

Old Mac was dead then.

Aunt Emily didn't say anything more about a miracle. But as Oliver, Hannah, and their parents left, she hugged each of them, and John Tate last. "I'm glad you're home, John," she said.

Oliver's father was anxious to see the other children, and Uncle Will offered to drive them home in his big sleigh.

Oliver would have liked for Bert to come with them, but he didn't say anything as he took his place in the corner of the back bench and pulled Uncle Will's buffalo robe over himself. Bert stood with his mother, shivering without a coat. Oliver felt shy about saying goodbye. He had so many questions he wanted to ask instead, like how did this change things? Because surely it did. It had to. Things couldn't be left as they'd been before the explosion.

The horses were anxious to be off after spending the morning in the barn behind the store, and now they pulled against Uncle Will's hold on the reins.

It was now or never. Oliver had to make a move. He looked directly at Bert. "I'll see you soon," he said softly, hoping that Bert would understand it to be a question.

"Yes," Bert answered.

As the horses strained forward, Oliver settled back under the buffalo robe, pulling it up until it tickled his nose. Maybe things weren't resolved in the way that he would like them to be, but at least he and Bert had an agreement; they would see each other.

Uncle Will turned the sleigh around the last turn to Oliver's home.

"My offer's still open, John," he said in a voice that was so low that Mum, in the other corner of the back bench with Hannah in her lap, couldn't hear. But Oliver could. He looked at his father.

Uncle Will must have meant the offer of Scrawny Joe's job at the dry goods store. Father didn't look at Uncle Will.

He looked at the trees they were passing. "I'm thinking about it, Will," he said.

They pulled up in front of the house. "I'll stop by the Krugers and see if Belle has returned home," Uncle Will said.

"I'll go with you, Uncle Will," Oliver said. "I was supposed to take care of Belle."

Uncle Will smiled. "That's all right, Oliver. You stay with your family. I'll let you know if anything is wrong."

"Thanks, Uncle Will."

"That would be kind," said Mum, as Father helped her out of the sleigh.

"It's good to be home," Father said to Uncle Will, and shook his brother's hand, holding it for a long moment before going into the house.

Eliza, Alberta, and Gavin were huddled in the middle of Mum's and Father's bed, surrounded by quilts and pillows. Eliza held the small collection of family photographs and was telling Alberta and Gavin family stories. "They were so afraid – I thought I ought to keep them busy," Eliza said, and Oliver saw that even though her hands shook she'd managed to hide her fear from her brother and sister.

"When the shaking and rumbling started we didn't know what it was. We crawled in here and stayed."

Alberta was busy pointing out something in a photograph to Gavin, and she was laughing as if nothing had happened.

Mr. Kruger knocked on the door early the next morning. Father answered, and Mr. Kruger held Father's hand firmly and shook it well. "Glad you're home, Tate," he said. "I was worried about you." Then he lowered his voice, but Oliver, standing in the loft almost directly over him, could hear every word. "You're not making plans to go back on one of those fool trips, are you?"

"I'm going to try again to find work. I don't want to go back, no." Father cleared his throat. "Actually, I'm considering another offer."

"Glad to hear it." Mr. Kruger finally released Father's hand and raised his voice to his normal level. "Where's that son of yours? I've a surprise for him."

Oliver backed away from where he crouched at the railed edge of the loft and climbed down the ladder as his father called his name.

"Belle is safe?" asked Oliver as he reached the floor.

"She's fine – although I'm not at all certain she wants to see you again!" Mr. Kruger smiled.

"She must have run straight home. The cutter needs a spot of work."

"I'll mend it," Oliver said quickly.

Mr. Kruger continued. "And after you've helped me with that, I thought I might help you make a sleigh."

"A sleigh, sir?" Oliver remembered Scrawny Joe's sleigh, and skimming over the ice. "I'd like a sleigh, but I haven't any means of using it. Especially now." He thought of Old Mac.

Mr. Kruger shook his head. "I think that'll change. My dog, Pepper, she's going to whelp a fine batch of pups this spring. And after she's nursed them for a time, they're yours."

Oliver looked at his father and tried not to sound too excited. "I'll have to talk about it with my father, Mr. Kruger," he said.

"Of course," said the farmer. "A dog team is a lot of work, but you can do it. Next winter – more likely the one following – you'll be racing between here and that cousin's place and turning figure eights on the ice."

Father spoke up. "Last night I heard the news that my son is something of a wage earner. So he can afford to keep the dogs if he wants to. Besides, we need some transport-ation."

"That's it, then!" Mr. Kruger smiled. "I too heard you're working for Mr. Campbell. Do you know that he saved young Rosie Flynn's life?"

Oliver shook his head, but in his mind he saw the face of the girl in the hotel window. Could it be?

Mr. Kruger was shaking his head. "Who would have thought he had it in him? Everyone's talking about it. No one else noticed her, it seems, but he dashed into the hotel and the windows had blown out right there! She might have bled to death if he hadn't carried her to the Doc's. Seems she was stunned – kept waving and saying she was fine, but she couldn't move!"

Oliver spoke up. "Mr. Campbell's a kind man underneath."

"Well, I'll be more inclined to believe that now," said Mr. Kruger, and he turned to leave.

"Mr. Kruger?" Oliver called. "Thank you, sir."

Mr. Kruger nodded, smiled, as he left.

"So," said Oliver's father. "You've gotten to know the blacksmith. He's a good man, to give you work."

"He is a good man. Others can see that now too." Oliver hesitated. "Father, I'd like to see Bert and tell him about the sleigh and dogs."

Surely this was reason to see Bert. Oliver couldn't wait to tell him. He put his jacket and snowshoes on and realized that he wasn't sure what excited him more: the prospect of his own dog team and sleigh or being able to tell the news to Bert.

He'd not gone far when he heard a shout

behind him. It was his father, his coat flapping open, his cap in hand.

"Wait, Oliver!" he called. "I'm coming with you." He caught up to where Oliver stood.

"I have to talk with your Uncle Will," he said.

"About the job?" asked Oliver bluntly.

His father looked surprised. Then he seemed to relax. "Yes – about the job."

Oliver reached for his father's hand and led the way towards the road. His father would have a difficult time trying to walk the trail without snowshoes.

"Are you going to take the job with Uncle Will?" he asked.

His father was silent for a minute until they were on the roadway, then his steps fell into a rhythm.

"I am – going to take the job. It'll mean moving into town," he said, glancing at Oliver.

"I know."

They walked on, and then Oliver asked: "Did you know that Uncle Will said you're stubborn and proud?"

Father nodded. "He told me so himself – and I think he might be quite close to the truth." He began to walk faster and Oliver followed.

Chapter 12

As Oliver and his father entered the Landing people were still cleaning up, using brooms to sweep the long spears and chips of glass from the street and clearing small trees and large branches that had been thrown into the air like twigs.

They made their way down the street between the bits of debris.

Uncle Will was busy in the store when Oliver crawled through the windowless door. Father reached in and unlocked the door himself, closing it carefully behind him so that the jagged pieces of glass wouldn't fall to the floor.

"Haven't even had time to fix my own door, I've been so busy." Uncle Will spoke as he walked towards them.

He had an enormous grin on his face. "Seems that this order of glass wasn't a mistake after all – sold almost every piece." His grin disappeared for a moment though. "Not that I would have wished this on anyone," he said. The grin reappeared. "Still, I didn't know how long it would take to clear the store of this shipment."

Oliver's father stared at Uncle Will for a moment. "Suppose I get started on the door," he said.

Uncle Will's grin stretched farther. "That would be good, John."

Uncle Will suddenly remembered Oliver. "I guess you'll be wanting Bert – he's upstairs." Uncle Will pointed as if Oliver had forgotten the way.

Oliver climbed the narrow stairs, thinking how strange it was that no one was speaking directly about the fights. Father had only said that he'd work on the door, which meant that he was going to work with Uncle Will in Prince Arthur's Landing, and all Uncle Will had said was, "That would be good, John."

And Mum hadn't even asked questions. Surely she and Aunt Emily must have talked. Aunt Emily might have even told her about Oliver's dinner with Mr. Campbell and Miss Darbyshire.

Maybe they were so glad the differences were over that they didn't want to talk about it. But it haunted Oliver. Why, he wasn't sure. Perhaps because it had happened so easily and perhaps it could happen again. He didn't want it to happen ever again.

Bert was waiting by the window in the front room for him. "I saw you coming down the street." He already had his outdoor clothes on. And mittens. Oliver's lost mittens. Bert looked rather sheepish as he realized that Oliver was staring at his hands.

"Here," he said quickly and pulled them off.

Oliver reached out for the mittens, then stopped. "No," he said, "you keep them. I knew you'd be able to find them, but I never had the courage to come and ask you."

Bert interrupted. "After you left I found them, one under the cedar trees and one on the street. I've worn them ever since. I kept thinking that I could use them as a reason to come and talk to you." He was still holding them out to Oliver, but Oliver pushed his hand away.

"No – keep them. Every time I see you wearing them I'll remember this time."

Bert pushed his fingers into the mittens and held up his hands.

"It's not going to happen again, is it?" said Oliver. "We can't fight like that, Bert."

Bert shook his head. "No, it's not going to happen again. And thanks for the mittens," he added.

"You're welcome. Mum made me these." Oliver wiggled his hands in the new bright red mitts.

Aunt Emily came to the door holding out a bulging sack. "Here's a winter picnic lunch. Now you two go before you have me in tears again. I've cried so much since New Year's Eve that I'm going to need more salt pork in my diet."

Bert raised his brows. "We'd best get out of here – Mum's been like the Kakabeka Falls lately."

Oliver and Bert set out for their special place without saying a word about their destination. They knew where they were going. Bert finally spoke as they neared the last curve in the path.

"I'm sorry about Old Mac," he said.

Oliver just nodded. He couldn't speak around the lump in his throat. Every time he thought of Mac he had to remind himself of the fact that the horse was responsible for saving his father. Oliver even liked to imagine that Old Mac had smelled the smoke from the fire and that was what had caused him to stop.

But he didn't say any of this to Bert. He just nodded and settled into a comfortable silence that lasted until they reached their place.

Mr. Campbell stood there as if he'd been waiting for them. "Thought I might find you here," he said. His usual grumpy face – the face that Oliver always thought of as his mask – didn't have its usual lines, and he appeared to be in good spirits.

"How'd he know about our place?" Bert

whispered to Oliver, who shrugged.

"I don't know – I never told him."

Mr. Campbell ignored their whisperings and continued. "It makes me gladden to see you two friends again. Aye, if it takes a blasted explosion and buildings disappearing in the air to bring you together, so be it." He reached into his shirt for his flask, but changed his mind and instead turned to point out to the bay.

"Look!" he cried. "The ice is broken."

The ice was broken. Enormous pieces of earth had been flung like sand into the Bay and had shattered the ice. Farther out, Oliver and Bert could see where it had given way completely to open water.

"Why, those pieces must weigh half a ton!" Mr. Campbell peered at Oliver. "I'd be willing to bet my boots you thought that ice could never break."

Oliver didn't answer. He stared out at the Bay for a long time. He didn't even notice when Mr. Campbell left, muttering about things breaking and mending.

"Mr. Campbell's right – I never thought the lake ice could be broken."

"That was some explosion," said Bert with a hushed voice.

"It's surprising what can be broken sometimes," Oliver said, speaking so softly that he wasn't certain if Bert could hear him.

"I guess anything can be broken," said Bert, and Oliver knew they weren't talking about the ice any more.

It was odd to see the open water at that time of year. It reminded Oliver of summertime, and the thought occurred to him that the water was always the same, whether under ice or not, and even as different currents and winds brought water from other parts of the changing world.

Oliver looked at Bert. He knew that both of them had changed in the past few weeks, but he also knew that what they cared for in each other would always be there. He would have to remind himself of that.

"I'm sorry I've been so stubborn." Oliver held his hand out to his cousin.

Bert took his hand and shook it firmly. "I'm sorry too," he said. Then he turned back to look at the Bay. He spoke as if to comfort Oliver. "This broken ice will melt and summer will come and next year the ice will be exactly the same."

"It will, won't it?" Oliver smiled, and they both watched as Mr. Meikle, the fancy skater, stepped out from the edge of the lake and slowly began to trace great loops and fine turns onto the ice, like map lines around the holes.

Afterword

A S MISS DARBYSHIRE PREDICTED, FORT WILLIAM and Prince Arthur's Landing did become one great city. (In 1883, the name of Prince Arthur's Landing was changed to Port Arthur; someone decided the Landing was too long to be written on railway signs and tickets.)

But it took time. For many years, Port Arthur and Fort William continued to be often at odds, and the two towns spread out and grew away from each other. Every so often, someone would mention the possibility of becoming one, but no one seemed to listen. At least, not seriously.

After World War II, the towns, now cities, began to decline. It was very costly to maintain two municipal halls, with two mayors and two councils, two fire and police departments, two transit systems ... two of everything. It became difficult to find work, so young adults left the area as they left home, and the population didn't grow. City officials and business people began to think that if the two cities shared their resources, their strengths, the area could grow.

On June 26, 1959, the St. Lawrence Seaway was officially opened, and this brought about the realization of a dream long held by both cities: a dream of ocean-going vessels being able to sail to the head of the lake. It also brought about a time of prosperity for both Port Arthur and Fort William.

On April 16, 1968, in a lecture hall at Lakehead University, a government official read a recommendation that the two cities become one as quickly as January 1, 1970. The two mayors were happy about the recommendation, but one MPP called for a referendum so that all the citizens could vote on the issue. The referendum never did take place, and many people were angry that they hadn't been able to vote. (Though 79% said, in a telephone survey, that they would have voted for the amalgamation.) But they felt forced to accept the government's decision, and it took several years and much wrangling for everyone to feel comfortable with the new Thunder Bay.

For the opening of 1970, the New Year celebration included a giant "Happy Birthday Thunder Bay" sign, as well as the firing of a dozen aerial bombs and church bells ringing. An "Ode to Thunder Bay" was played by the

McGillivray Pipe Band and the mayor broke a bottle of champagne with a broad axe.

The Old Fort was rebuilt in 1973 and the reconstruction seemed to cause people to forget their differences and to remember their history, and they began to feel pride in what they shared.

So a New Year opened this story, and a New Year opened the story of Thunder Bay as a joined city. A city that is now one and strong at the head of Lake Superior.